Ack

MW01152725

I give thanks and must express the deepest appreciation from the bottom of my heart and the depths of my soul to The Most High, My Family, Friends, Supporters and YOU the reader. I value your time and attention.

Please Do The Following

1) Subscribe to the Brother Dash email list for free downloads and info on new books by visiting www.brotherdash.com.
2) Post a review of the novel on your favorite sites and post feedback on the author's site.
3) Follow @brotherdash on all relevant social media
4) Share a photo with you and the book, your book club, or a selfie with the author on your own social media

To Learn More About Brother Dash

Visit: www.brotherdash.com
Email: dash@brotherdash.com

Please share links to the novel on your social media
&
Happy Reading

The Donor

When Conception Meets Deception

A Romantic Suspense

Brother Dash

Table of Contents

I Run This City

❧

"Shauntelle? What are you doing here? Where's your sister?" he says.

Shauntelle freezes on the top step of the stoop and screws her eyebrows down at him. She hoists a hefty bag on her shoulder and elbows past him toward an idling minivan.

"Shauntelle. Shauntelle, I'm talking to you. Where's your sister?"

"I don't got shit to say to you and neither does my sister."

Her chocolate arms dump the heavy plastic bag in the backseat. A pair of her sister's jeans flop out. His eyes pop. As he turns to bolt up the steps, a teary eyed woman appears in the doorway.

"Babe, babe what are you doing?" he says.

The woman ignores him and clanks an overstuffed suitcase out of the Brooklyn brownstone.

"Babe, stop. I asked you a question."

He grabs her arm. She glares back. Her hazel brown eyes are pink and puffy. She blinks with a sniffle and a trickle.

"Get your paws off of me," she says.

"Babe, listen. I know you're upset. Let me ex—,"

"Negro, please," Shauntelle says. "Get out of my sister's way."

The woman snatches her arm from his grip. She rolls the suitcase to the curb. He fires a stiff finger at Shauntelle.

"Mind your damn business, Shauntelle. This is between us."

Shauntelle looks him up and down. Then she gets up in his face.

"I always knew you was hiding something. Ain't *no* man *that* damn perfect."

Her sister stomps back toward the steps. He blocks her.

"Baby, please. What you heard isn't the whole truth."

"You're in my way," she says.

"Baby, at least let me try to—"

"Move," she says.

The nosy neighbor from across the street bends her ear to the action. She continues to sweep her porch. It's immaculate.

"Sweetheart, don't act this way. That's not how we do," he says. His lady shoots her arms to the sky.

"How *we* do? What *we* are you talking about? I don't know you anymore. I never did. You were nothing but a lie. You played me for a fool. I wasted four years of my life on your lying ass. Four years."

"Mmmhmm that's right sis, you tell him. He ain't shit [she turns to him]. You know you ain't shit right?"

"Bud out, Shauntelle...Now babe, please. I can explain."

"Don't touch me," she says.

"Sweetheart you don't understand. This whole day has been the day from hell for me."

"For *you*? Are you serious? You have no idea what you put me through do you? Do you? I gave you my heart, my soul, my body. I promised myself to you. I let you put this damn rock on my finger. And you were nothing but a fake."

"Fraudulent...Bitch. Ass. Liar," Shauntelle says. She screws her index finger into his temple. He *shoulder-shrugs* it from his face.

Shauntelle's sister cuts in.

"I had to find out about you at my law firm? In front of all of the partners? My colleagues?"

"Babe, I-I-I'll make this right. I'll tell them you knew nothing about this. I don't want you to get fired for my mistake."

CLAP CLAP CLAP Shauntelle claps in his face.

"Hey, dummy. It's bad either way. Either she knew about your shit—which makes her a trifling ass liar like you—or she *didn't* know about your shit—I repeat—*YOUR* muthafuckin' shit, which means she got played by a player. That would make her boo-boo the fool. So since you wanna be out here *explaaainin'* shit. Explain that one, *bruh.*"

He scans the treelined block. The commotion has brought several neighbors out of their homes. He leans into his lady's ear and says, "Can we discuss this inside please?"

"Oh hell no. No, no, no," she says, with a finger wag. "You don't get to keep hiding. You destroyed my world. Why do you get to keep yours a secret?"

"You tell him sis," Shauntelle says.

He grits his teeth and side-eyes her.

"Don't look at me like you fittin' to do something. 'Cause ya' ain't."

"Listen, babe. I-I messed up. But this has all been a big—"

"A big what? Misunderstanding? Mistake? Oh wait. Let me guess. It's a conspiracy. Have you forgotten that I'm a lawyer? I've heard it all."

"Actually, it kind of is all of those things if you would just—"

"Oh my God. This punk bitch here," Shauntelle says, tossing her hands in the air. "Sis, let's get the rest of your stuff and leave this clown on the street with the rest of the trash."

Shauntelle pushes him aside and scoots up the steps. Her brokenhearted sister hurries up the stoop behind her.

"Babe wait. Babe"—he drops to his knees—"Please. Baby I love you."

She pauses at the top. Stiffens her arms. Clenches her fists. And pivots in slow motion.

"You *love* me? What do you know about love?…Answer me."

"Babe, I—"

"Love? Love is when a woman's heart opens from a man's smile. Love is when she ignores her eyes and believes his tongue."

"Lucifer!" Shauntelle shouts.

"Love is having to tolerate catcalls all day but getting to come home to a man that respects you…cradles you…protects you at night. Love is knowing he'll always want to dance to the music in our heads, lock pinkies through Central Park, grow old and grey on a porch. I thought you knew how to love. No. You only know how to hurt."

She hovers above as he remains on bent knees. Her eyes burn with the heat of boiled tears. Without hesitation he leaps to his feet. He seizes her shoulders and forces a kiss. She squirms and wriggles in his vise-like clutch. He sticks his tongue into her resistant mouth.

"Mmph. Argh. Ugh. Mmph," she protests. His lips refuse to release their lock.

Shauntelle comes bounding down the steps towards her sister but before she could interrupt, he screams in pain and grabs his mouth.

"Ow. Argh. " He hunches over. A drop of blood drips from his split tongue.

"You bih me," he slobbers, unable to pronounce the t.

"That's right girl bite him. Bite his ass. Crunch that shit," Shauntelle says. "Oh you thought you was gonna shove your nasty, lying tongue down my sister's throat and she was just gonna melt in your mouth? Why? 'Cause you said, *I love you?* Well you done learned today didn't ya'? How your tongue feel now, mumble mouth?"

Salty rivers flow down his cheeks. His lips part for the only words he can muster…

"But I love you."

Those three words ignite her ire. She paces up and down the rough concrete. Arms flailing. Head pounding. Tears overflowing.

"I *hate* you. I hate you. I hate you. You humiliated me. You hurt me. You destroyed *us.* You ripped my heart out. I-I-I can't think. I-I can't talk. I can't breathe. I-I-…You know what? Forget it. Keep whatever is left in that house. Keep it all. I can't stand the sight of you. I can't stand the smell of you. I can't stand the taste of you."

HACH-TUCH-SPIT

She spits in his face. Shauntelle smirks with pride.

The thick glob slugs down his cheek. He doesn't wipe it off. As she trembles, Shauntelle rushes to her aid. She smoothes her palm over her sister's cries. And kisses her forehead.

"Shhhh. It's okay sis. You gonna be alright. I got you. Come on. Let's go home."

Shauntelle braces her sister by the shoulder and ushers her into the passenger seat of the minivan. She hops in the driver's seat. They drive up the block but as they approach the stop sign, Shauntelle pauses at the corner. She shifts into reverse. His heart smiles with hope as the van returns. He rushes towards the passenger door. The love of his life rolls down the window…leans out, and throws a perfect strike that clinks off his forehead. He looks at the pavement. The afternoon sun shimmies off the diamond engagement ring. It has just landed in a hot pile of dog shit. Shauntelle leans from the driver's seat to make eye contact with him. She sucks her teeth and gives him the finger. Her sister buries her face in her palms. And with that…the van *vrooms* up the street…it turns the corner…and she's gone.

This is where we are now. But it is not where we should begin. For that we must go back. Back to where it all started. On a famous bridge. In a town called Brooklyn…

❧

9 Months Ago

Gotham. They say she never sleeps. And on this night, neither does he. The thick choke of muggy air wrestles him from a restless slumber. It stirs and spurs him for a third consecutive midnight run towards...*the city*. Manhattan. Puckered lips suck air and blow out. *HUH, PAT PAT...HUH, PAT PAT...HUH, PAT PAT.* Every limb and ligament lunges toward the slender buildings with the bright lights. The sweat of his bulging quads, and chiseled calves, lotion his skin to a moonlit mocha. With his Brooklyn brownstone now several blocks behind, he crosses the bridge.

At this early hour Wall Street's sidewalks are empty. His meaty muscles stroke and strike the asphalt. He winces from the exhaust of an idling yellow taxi. Eventually, weariness takes over and he slows to a stop at Water Street. White steam bellows from street sewers. His hands choke his knees. His cheeks pulse as his chest heaves for city oxygen. As salty sweat seeps into the grooves of his parched lips he gets that tingle. It's the sensation you get when you feel you're being watched.

"Well ain't that a plump rump," a raspy voice says.

It startles him. He darts and dips but all he sees is a boarded row of storefronts.

"Don't look around all strange," the female voice says. "With your hot and sweaty self. Looking all delicious with them tight green shorts. Like a candy apple Jolly Rancher."

The voice has a Georgia drawl. It's coming from the musty vestibule of a shuttered bodega. He crouches and follows the sound into the shadows. His gaze is met by a pair of pupils. A woman's face emerges from the dank corner. Stringy follicles droop over her wrinkled brow. She smiles. The few teeth she has left dangle from her black gums. Like loose window shutters. A dozen glass bottles stand in military rows by her pink ankles. And she smells like poultry.

"Be still in the light so I can sees you. Damn. A strong strapping man. All buff puffed up. My old man used to pump iron too."

He rises from his knees.

"Oooh you's a tall one. How tall is you?"

"About six three," he replies.

"Six foot three? Oh no, no. He wasn't that damn tall. And you more milk chocolate than he was. He was more high yella. Like Al B. Sure or that green-eyed Michael…um…what's his name? Michael Easy."

"I think you mean Michael Ealy," he says.

"Shiny bald head too. Lookin' tasty." She turns to converse with her bottles. "You know something y'all? That's what I need. A strong, tasty man. Like this here buff puff." She snaps her fingers quickly. "You got a woman?"

She doesn't look up from the bottles.

"Uhhh, I think I should get back."

"What you runnin' fo' this time of night anyway? I mean I ain't complainin'. I'm enjoying the show." She winks with a cackle.

"Well…running helps me clear my mind."

"Awww, come sit next to Miss Pat, Buff Puff. I'll get that mind all cleared up," she says.

"Actually, I need to get going."

"Going? How you gonna leave without at least tellin' an old lady your name? Unless you prefer, Buff Puff?"

"You can stick with my name. It's Chase. Chase Archibald."

"Chase? Your Mama named you that? What kind of name is Chase? And what's that other part? Ar-Chee-Ball?"

She starts bobbing her head back-and-forth and singing his name.

Chase sprouts a look that says, *this lady cray cray*, and backs away.

She fires her a stiff palm like a traffic cop.

"Stop," she orders. "One more question."

Chase is more amused than disturbed so indulges her.

"Okay, Miss Pat. But just *one* more question."

"Okay. So your name is Chase, right?"

Chase nods.

"And you out here running, right?…So, let me ask you…is you the one doing the chasing or is you *being* chased?"

Chase pauses as he ponders. She asks a good question. He bends at the knee and replies in her bloodshot eyes with a single word…

"Yes."

Miss Pat curls her orange and grey eyebrows. But after a few seconds she shrugs her twiggy shoulders and returns to her captive audience of bottle people. Chase rises and gallops back towards, and over, the Brooklyn Bridge. He retraces his strides to the treelined streets of Cobble Hill and wonders if he is indeed running to something or running away from something…or *someone*.

⚜

In a Midwood, Brooklyn lecture hall, a creative writing class is under fire.

"Am I boring you Mr. Jankovic?" Professor Chase Archibald says."

"Huh? Who? Me? Yes?" the young student says.

"Yes? So I *am* boring you?" Chase asks.

"No. No, I mean—"

"No? Yes? You mean? Which is it young man?"

"No, I'm sorry Dr. Archibald."

"Not every professor is a doctor," Chase says.

"Oh-uh-sorry, *Professor* Archibald."

"Don't apologize to me Mr. Jankovic. Apologize to your fellow scholars. Your colleagues on the journey."

Chase directs his attention toward another student. "And what journey might that be Ms...[he scans the roster sheet]...Amendola?"

"Um," she says.

"Are you sure you want to start with *um*?" Chase asks.

"No, Professor," the young woman says.

Chase points across the lecture hall.

"Help them Ms. Ross-Jenkins."

"You asked about the journey, Professor. Is it the journey of...of knowledge?"

"Are you asking or telling?...Well? Tick-tock, tick-tock, come on now, Ms. Ross-Jenkins. We're on a sinking ship and you're the captain. Who can help her?"

Silence.

"Come on people think about what we just read."

Chase's scarlet and blue tie pokes from the crevice of his chestnut tweed vest. He drums his fingers on his shoulder. His eyes sweep the rows. Chase's mission is to whip these undergraduate creatives into shape through training, inspiration and a dose of compassion. The young Robbie Jankovic had the misfortune of being caught daydreaming. Chase uses this as a teachable moment. He beats an open palm against the lapel of his vest. The sound mimics the *THUMP-THUMP* of a heartbeat. He fires questions.

"What is Mr. Jankovic feeling right now Gina Amendola?"

BUP-BUP...BUP-BUP

"Anxiety?" Gina replies.

"Good. Now, Ross-Jenkins, you. Same question…but give me a simile. Let's go, chop-chop."

"He-he's nervous…nervous like…like he's being stalked in the woods by a serial killer," she says.

Gina jumps back in.

"Yeah. And it's a killer who tracks human prey by following the odor of their nervous sweat."

"Okay…now raise the stakes," Chase says.

"And it's summer," Ross-Jenkins says.

Chase increases the beats and pounds his chest with ferocity.

"During a heat wave," Gina says.

"And the killer stripped Robbie down to his nasty skivvies so his flesh is bared open, pink and naked and nasty and—"

"Okay, okay ladies. We won't build out that particular visual. But I love the creepy factor."

Chase grabs one of the metal folding chairs from behind the lectern. He creaks it open and swivels it around in front of Robbie. He straddles the seat and restarts the chest beat.

"Now back to you Mr. Jankovic. How do you feel?"

"Like I shouldn't have sat in the first row."

The class snickers.

"That's always the best seat in the house. Now describe your feeling with a creative use of danger. Be unique. Specific."

"I feel. I feel tense…um…with my guts like…" Chase eggs him on with a slow encouraging wave. "…tense with my guts like…like there's a bowl of burning hot mushy spaghetti in front of me, and there's a man with a gun to my head and if I want to live I have to untangle all of it…with my bare hands…in sixty seconds!"

Chase beams.

"Hooray. Excellent. Excellent. You see that class? Mr. Jankovic used temperature, texture and fear. As writers you need to tap into your own creative reservoir of emotion. And why is that Ms. Shah?"

She trembles.

"Well, I guess—"

"Don't guess, Ms. Shanti Shah. Be confident...*know*."

"We tap into our own emotions because you can't write what a character feels, if you don't *feel* yourself?"

The class clown Raymond Raymond [his real name] can't resist.

"Yo I feel you on that 'cause sometimes I likes to feel myself."

He rubs over his own chest and makes a duck face. The class roars. Chase is unamused.

"You know that is a fascinating bit of knowledge Mr. Raymond. Why don't you write a 5,000 word essay this weekend on character development. And present it to the class next week?"

"Oh uh—nah Mr. Archi—I mean *Professor* Archibald I'm good on that.," he stammers.

"No, no, Mr. Raymond. I insist. Ya' *feels* me, yo?" Chase says.

"Busted," Shanti says.

The class goes *Ooooh* and the wide-eyed comedian slumps in his chair.

"Okay, everyone. Just like the heartbeat I simulated from Edgar Allan Poe's *The Tell Tale Heart* I want you to consider how the five senses, such as sound, can help you create tension in a story. And remember this theme: Whenever you try to run from yourself, it is your *self* that will always catch up. Now scram. Go play in traffic. Class dismissed."

Books shut. Mobiles switch on. The entire hall clears as students hurry through the exit at the top of the stairs. Except for one female straggler seated in the top row. She rises. She sports a black skirt suit with lilac pinstripes over a size eight hourglass figure. Chase takes no notice of her as he gathers his papers and books from the grey folding table. She sideways shuffles down the row. She clutches a large purple suede bag against her hip. It is the kind of accessory created for women who prefer laptop bags that don't actually *look* like laptop bags. Her four inch red bottoms put her a wisp below six feet. She peers down the long aisle at the professor. He doesn't look up. She removes a crystal vial of gloss from her bag. She puckers, paints and pops her full lips to a juicy sheen. And then she slinks towards Chase, one seductive step at a time.

The hall's eighteenth century gothic windows wrap her in a hazy sunlight. She is a voluptuous silhouette. Chase finally glances. Her green, minty brown eyes smile at him. He ignores her. She continues to saunter in the empty room as if she were on a catwalk. She reaches him. Her french manicured fingernail crawls down the taut crease of her bosom stopping at the triangle of her blouse. *POP* goes the first button. But her bold cleavage elicits zero acknowledgement. She places her hand on her hip, screws her bottom lip and bangs her bag on his table. Chase shuffles his papers.

"Professor Archibald," she bellows.

"Ms. Dixon," he says, eyes still lowered.

She circles behind the table and cozies next to him.

"So, I have a question,"she says.

"Questions are for my office hours on Tuesdays, Ms. Dixon. That was in the syllabus on day one."

"Well, I'm not waiting until next week for an answer Professor Archibald."

Citrus and patchouli snake from her neck to his nostrils. The aroma is a fishhook drawing his gaze to hers. She slides her light mocha fingers inside the crease of his vest and squeezes a pec. He gulps.

"We discussed your impetuousness before, Ms. Dixon."

He squirms away.

"Get back here," she says, and clutches his chin.

"Ms. Dixon. This behavior of yours. You can't—mmph".

Mmph. She pulls his mouth to hers and opens. Her tongue slaps inside his cheeks like a wet palm on a conga drum. Chase's chest surges into Dixon's firm C-cups. His resistance has become futile. He grabs her ample posterior and lifts her onto the folding table. He pokes his finger under the front clasp of her bra strap and frees the contents. Long, strong, thick fingers ski up and down her cinnamon brown hills. Their tongues leap and dive in their mouths. They come up for air only for naughty small talk.

"Ooh…you're being very…mmm….oh…so…mmmhmm… inappropriate, Ms. Dixon."

"So why don't you *appropriate* me, professor?"

Chase takes her question as a command. He hoists her in the air so she straddles him. Her red bottom heels dangle. The hem of her skirt rises up her thighs. The muscular intellectual braces her with ease. They *froggy-hop* to the podium and back to the table. He lays her on her back and splays her legs open.

"Am I still being inappropriate professor?"

"*Very,*" he says.

He gnarls his hungry eyes at her open blouse. Ms. Dixon bites her bottom lip with a smile. She grabs his belt, hurries with the unbuckling and pulls his wool trousers down. He hovers over her, climbs on top of the table, pulls down her purple panties and—

"Ahem," gargles a throat from the top step.

Chase freezes his stare up and to the right. His mouth drops in horror.

"D-D-Dean Ganges," he says.

Brooklyn University Dean and Chair of the English Department, Dr. Octavia Ganges glares down from the highest row of the lecture hall. But as she does so, the folding table starts to tremble from the weight of two bodies. The metal rods creak before a loud…*BOOM!*

The table collapses. Ms. Dixon flails like an overturned beetle. Chase attempts to stand. Her toe catches him between his legs.

"Arrgh," he says, and grabs the swollen arc of his loin.

Chase is a disheveled mess. He tries to explain himself as he hurriedly buckles his trousers and tucks in his shirt.

"Uh-uh-um…see…uh."

Dean Ganges folds her arms and strokes her chin.

"Would you like a towel for that sloppy mouth as well Professor Archibald?" she says.

"Sloppy mouth?" Chase says with a back palm wipe of his wet lips. "Um no ma'am. I mean yes. I mean…."

"Well which is it? No? Yes?" she says, as she bobs and weaves like Muhammad Ali.

Ms. Dixon however isn't frazzled. She calmly fastens her lavender and lace bra and buttons her blouse.

Dean Ganges trots down the steps and halts in front of Chase. Her stout, four foot eleven inch frame is elegant but authoritative. She wears an amber pant suit. It compliments her dark chocolate skin. Due to her smooth, *black don't crack* flawlessness, she appears two decades younger than her sixty-something years would indicate. Chase wrings his wrists.

"Nothing to say Professor?" she says.

"I-I-I," he stutters.

Her dimpled, globe cheeks snark with a deceptive smile.

"Oh my. He sure is squirming isn't he Ms. Dixon?"

"Well, I heard you have that effect on men, Octavia."

"Girl you ain't never lie," Dean Ganges replies.

The two women grab their bellies in laughter before wrapping one another in a familiar embrace.

"Girl, it's been months since I've seen you. How has Attorney Jenae Dixon been?" Dean Ganges says.

"I've been good Octavia. How's your English department?" Jenae asks.

"Not bad. Just the occasional bratty, priveleged student or a frisky, six foot three professor...with his fly still open."

Chase turns around to zip up.

"What brings you by today?" Dean Ganges asks.

"One of my clients had a complaint with the probation office on Nostrand and Flatbush Avenue. I reminded them about New York State penal code and department policies regarding treatment towards ex-offenders. So since I was in the neighborhood—"

"—You decided to drop in on tricky dicky over here," Dean Ganges says.

Jenae laughs.

"Octavia you're a mess. It's just that this past summer was so hectic for Chase and I. He taught summer sessions, I was back and forth to our D.C. office. And then there's the young man Chase mentors most weekends from the group home. We haven't seen much of each other lately. So I thought I'd surprise my handsome, professor boyfriend by slipping in the back and catching the remainder of his lecture."

Jenae strokes Chase's cheeks.

Chase clears his throat.

"Dean Ganges I must apologize."

"Chase, it's okay. Jenae is quite the temptress. Especially in that incredible, courtroom winning *en-sem-blay*. Girl, I need that outfit. But only if they make it in petite divalicious? 'Cause you know these hips bring the all the boys to the yard, girl."

She slides her gem studded fingers over her curves and twirls for effect.

"Octavia, I can't with you," Jenae chuckles. "But listen, I do need to get going. Two errands and then I have to stop at *Junior's*. You know a sister been fiending for some *Junior's* cheesecake all day."

Jenae bends down to kiss the diminutive Dean Ganges goodbye.

"Actually, I'll walk out with you," the Dean says.

Jenae smoothes her hand on Chase's chest and gives him a peck.

"I'll text you later babe," she says.

The two women walk up the carpeted steps. As they reach the exit, Chase yells up.

"Dean Ganges. Didn't you stop for something?"

"It can wait until next week's department meeting," she says.

"Are you sure, Dean? I mean we can—"

"No, it's fine lover boy. But next time save the kinky adventures with your girlfriend for your office. With the door *locked*."

"Dean Ganges I'm so sorry. We can talk about—"

"Oh relax. Next week, next week," she says.

"But—"

She flips her hand as if she were shooing a fly. As the two women exit the room arm-in-arm, Chase hears them burst into a roaring cackle as their heels click-clack down the hallway.

He sighs with nervous relief and gathers his papers and books. He attempts to stand the table erect again but the mangled metal is a lost cause. He tightens his necktie, checks he has his MetroCard for the subway, and composes a quick text to Jenae as he walks out:

```
Babe you been running around all day. I'll
    stop at Juniors for you. Come over
        2nite. I'll cook. And feed you
   cheesecake for dessert. With my fingers.
                  :)
              #LuvMeSumYou
```

The stodgy hall is now empty. But not quiet. A series of touchtone beeps echo from the room's *other* exit. There's a door behind the podium and it had been wedged open—by just a crack—this entire time. A tall, giant of a man pokes his head inside. He puts the phone to his ear and waits for it to answer.

Yeah, the voice on the other end says.

"It's me," the man says.

Why do you always announce yourself? Phones have caller i.d.

"Sorry, boss."

So, what's the deal? Is it him?

"I think so. He's the right height. I'm six foot seven and he comes to my nose. Looks alot like the picture you gave me too."

Good. What else you find out?

"He's got a woman. Some lawyer. His boss walked in so now I know her name and what she looks like."

Good. That could be useful. Get more info on the chick and the boss. Update me in two days.

"Cool. Oh and boss, one more thing. Kind of weird but they kept calling him something else. Somebody named Chase Archibald."

*Chase Archibald? Hah. **That's** the name he picked?*

2 Bedroom.Baller

❧

A crisp autumn breeze slips between the bedroom's cherrywood shutters. It sails over the melted soy candles perched atop the birch dresser. A powdery trail of ashes collect in the groove of a wooden incense holder. The faint aroma of Nag Champa—and midnight copulation—lingers like the dancing limbs of drunk lovers.

Jenae slumbers on the sable silk sheets. Wind and sun caress her golden brown nakedness. The street sounds of bike pedals and cars clunking over potholes are drowned out by the shower in the master bath. After two squeaks of the hot and cold handles, the *SWOOSH* of water subsides. Chase reenters the room. Nude. Hot mist trails from his skin like pulled cotton. He drip-drops across the alpaca rug and smiles at the mattress. His gaze caresses her sienna twists, smooth shoulders and toned arms. He drinks in her ample thighs and bulbous bottom. But it is not her ravishing physique nor the memory of last night's pleasure that brightens his face. It is simply...her. His woman. His lover. His friend. Perhaps sensing his presence she rolls over and stretches a sleepy good morning yawn.

"Mmm, well good morning Mister Clean," Jenae says.

Startled, Chase snatches the plush cotton towel from his neck and snugs it around his waist. He marches to the dresser.

"Oh honey, I don't know why you always get shy like this. Over three years together you don't have anything I haven't already seen and felt and tasted. Like last night, and last week in the lecture hall, and the other day at—"

"We're not even going to bring up the lecture hall again. I was so embarrassed. In front of Dean Ganges? My boss? Most people would consider that a fireable offense."

"Chase, Octavia told me later that she was watching us for a good two minutes before she cleared her throat. I think she enjoyed the peep show."

"She what?" Chase freezes one leg through a pair of boxers.

"Oh, you're so cute when you turn into a prude."

Jenae slinks out of bed and sashays to him. She massages his firm shoulders. His boxers drop. She glides an open palm across the razor stubble below his navel. Chase whirls her around, grapples her pear bottom and seals her mouth with his kiss.

"*Mmph*, Chase, *mmph*, babe, wait, *mmph*, I haven't brushed yet. I still have morning brea—*Mmmmm*".

Her hands course up his neck and grip his bald held. Chase lifts and lays her on the bed. Chase's skin is still wet. But now it's hot. He pulls her knees apart and rubs the bottom ridge of his thick stiffness up her moist warmth. She shivers with a twitch of electricity and sits up on her elbows. She licks her tongue between her teeth. Her seductive sneer suggests she has another thought in mind.

"Stand up," she commands.

"You're about to get naughty aren't you?" Chase says.

She pumps her eyebrows.

Jenae hops off the bed and presses her mouth to his chest. She laps her tongue down his hard abs toward the middle of his pelvis. But he halts her descent with a gentle finger tug on her chin. Jenae's eyebrows contort with confusion. He makes them switch positions. It is *he*, that drops to *his* knees and paints a masterpiece on her body with his tongue. He mouths and sucks and kisses every cave, curve, and crevice. He leaves blush stained marks on her nutmeg skin.

Hickies are the graffiti of lovers. He stands her up and licks the insides of her thighs. Her legs buckle.

"Oooh…Chase," she says.

She tries to fall back onto the bed but he keeps her erect. He hovers his gaping mouth between her legs and huffs two hot breaths on her tingling center.

"Oh my God," she whimpers.

He keeps huffing and blowing but won't do what she wants him to do. She clutches the back of his head and pulls but he jerks back. She grits her teeth in frisky frustration.

"Chase, you're teasing."

"Do you want me?" he says.

"Yes."

"I can't hear you, Jenae."

"Yes, Yes. Chase, baby please."

"I'm not convinced."

"Chase!" she yells.

Chase ends her sensual torture. He grabs her hips, opens wide and slips his thick, sloppy tongue insi—

KNOCK KNOCK KNOCK

"Chase…Eh yo Chase you in here?" a young voice says at the bedroom door.

The bedroom door starts to creaks open.

"Chase I'm coming in."

"Whoa, wait, wait," both Chase and Jenae shout.

Jenae and Chase rush toward the closet but stumble over each other and fall.

"You a'ight Chase? I'm coming in, okay?"

"No!" Chase and Jenae yell.

"Babe, what time is it?" Chase whispers.

Jenae shrugs in annoyance as she rifles through the closet. Chase grabs his workout gear.

"How did he get inside and up the stairs? You gave him a key?"

"No, of course not. But I totally lost track of the time. I must have been distracted, hee hee."

"Yeah, yeah. Whatever."

She squeezes into a crisp new pair of black, Ralph Lauren jeans.

The voice yells through the crack of the door.

"Come on Chase. Them other dudes gonna get the court like the last time you was late. Then we gonna have to wait behind like a gazillion million other squads."

"Gimme a sec Devantay...Babe, toss me that clean basketball shirt please."

"Oooh, you got a female in there?"

"Quiet, little man. Jenae's here. Stop being a nosy twelve year old," Chase says.

"*Heeey* Miss Jenae," Devantay says through the door jam.

"Hello Devantay," Jenae yells back. She shoots a stern stare at Chase. "You *sooo* owe me for how you left me standing, you teaser."

She fluffs her soft natural curls in the mirror with a wire red, black and green afro pick...the one with the power fist.

They inspect their appearances. Chase opens the bedroom door. The shoulder high Devantay stands grinning as if he knows he interrupted two consenting adults. Under his armpit is the Spalding basketball Chase bought him last week.

"Hi, Miss Jenae."

"Hello Devantay," she replies.

Devantay's eyes circle the cavernous bedroom.

"Dang, Chase you got a phat room yo. I could be straight flossin' in this spot. For real, for real," he says.

"Get back in the hallway little man. This room is off limits to anyone not named, Jenae Monique Dixon."

Chase escorts Devantay out of the bedroom and down the spiral steps. They walk down the hallway—which was decorated by Jenae. She painted the walls crimson and cream with recessed shelves for Senegalese baskets and ebony-wood sculptures of Kenyan lovers with interlocking limbs. Devantay glances at the framed parchment with Arabic script. It was gifted to Chase by an older, bald-headed mentor. The translation reads:

> *There is no superiority of one race over another. God distinguishes humankind only by righteousness and good deeds.*

They head into the first floor living room.

"Devantay, how did you get in?" Chase asks.

"I don't know, I didn't break in," Devantay says—sounding like someone who *did* break in.

"I know you didn't *break* in. Wait, did I actually leave my door unlocked in the middle of Brooklyn?"

Devantay rubs his basketball and fidgets.

"I-I-I don't know. I mean it wasn't open, per see."

"Per see?" Chase says. "Oh you mean *per sé*."

"Right, per sé," Devantay says.

"Okay, so what does *that* mean?"

"Oh I know. It means it wasn't *open* open."

"Stop bouncing that ball in here. And I know the definition of the phrase I'm asking you how you got in my house?"

"I didn't break in okay?"

"Devantay, we have already established that…So?"

"So um, I…"

"Come on already."

Devantay's eyes well up. The nervous youth hyperventilates the way children do when forced to explain themselves.

"Chase, it's not like before. I'm not doing that no more. I'm not sneaking into people houses and stuff."

Devantay pokes his bottom lip. Chase can feel how upset Devantay is getting and stops his unintended interrogation.

"Hey, hey it's okay. I'm not upset. Come here little man…chin up."

Chase sits him on the walnut reading chair near the fireplace. He kneels in front of him and reassures the boy with a softer tone.

"I trust you Devantay. You've come a long way. But sometimes people backslide. They take two steps forward and then one step back. But that's alright. You won't get in trouble. So…did you take a step back? Did you pick the lock again?"

"No, no I didn't. I swear I didn't. Chase really, really, really, I—"

"Shh, shhh it's okay, it's okay. I believe you," Chase says. He hugs Devantay. "So, how *did* you got in, then?"

"I just turned the knob. I knocked a bunch of times but when you didn't answer I walked in. But I didn't break in Chase. I didn't."

"Okay, okay you can chillax," Chase says.

"Chillax? You old has heck. Nobody says chillax no more."

"*Any*more. And stay focused."

"You not gonna report me to Mr. James are you?"

Chase holds Devantay's hand.

"What? You're my dude. I'm not going to go running to the program director at the group home. Snitches get stitches right?" Chase winks and high fives him. "Just don't go walking all the way up into my bedroom next time."

Devantay chuckles.

"Got it," Devantay says.

"Let me just grab some hydration for us from the kitchen, and we can go school these suckers on the basketball court," Chase says.

"Dope. Oh, is your friend coming too?" Devantay says.

"My friend? What friend?" Chase says, grabbing two water bottles.

"The tall, fat guy. The one who kept asking me questions on the stoop."

"Huh? You kind of should have led with that one, Devantay."

Chase runs towards the door followed by the boy. They scoot past the poster prints on the kitchen wall: Muhammad Ali menacing over a fallen Sonny Liston, Jesse Owens in Berlin, Serena Williams with a bicep flex at Wimbledon. Chase holds his palm to his brow like a visor as he stands outside the 19th century double doors of the brownstone. He scans the neighborhood for the trespasser. Hipsters walking dogs, his nosy neighbor Mrs. Mahone sweeping her always clean cement porch, but no fat man.

"Do you see him Devantay?"

"Nope. But he was standing right there. He wasn't your friend?"

"A fat guy you say?" Chase asks.

"Yeah."

"*Yes*, not yeah," Chase admonishes.

"Yes," Devantay says.

"What did he say?"

"He said, 'Hey kid, you're Devantay aren't you?'"

"He knew your name?"

"Yeah. I mean yes. That's why I thought he was your friend. But I don't remember him from nowhere. I mean dude was huge. Like Rick Ross I'm a boss, I'm a boss, I'm a boss." He starts dancing and bobbing his shoulders.

"Devantay!"

"Oh, my bad."

"What else did he say?"

Chase continues to survey the block.

"Ugh. Chase we gonna miss reserving the dang court."

"First of all, watch your tone. And we'll be fine."

Chase hears footsteps approaching from inside.

"Oooh, shhh Devantay. Jenae's coming. Keep this between us."

Jenae walks through the glass and oak doors. She squints and then shields her eyes from the sudden blast of sunlight.

"What are my two handsome men shushing about?"

They remain silent.

Jenae side-eyes Devantay. He responds with the rapid fire reply of a child caught hiding a cookie.

"N-N-Nothin'. We wasn't talking about nothing."

Chase interrupts.

"Hey, honey. Me and little man have a game to get—"

"You hush, Chase," she says.

She points and curls a finger at Devantay.

He remains frozen at the front gate.

"Devantay?" she warns.

He complies. Jenae comforts his shoulders with her palms.

"Now you know I'm a lawyer right?"

"Yes."

"And what do lawyers do?"

"Scare little boys?"

Chase busts a belly laugh. Jenae winnows her eye at him.

"Now you look here, child. I have some questions for you," she says, mocking anger.

"Aww man. *More* questions? Ugh," Devantay says.

"More? What do you mean more?" she asks.

"Chase already asked me a bunch of questions about the fat ma —"

"Boy!" Chase yells.

"Devantay," Jenae purrs.

Chase cozies up behind Jenae. He attempts to distract her with soft pecks on her earlobe.

"That might have worked earlier," Jenae says. She slinks out of Chase's embrace. "Now what's this about a man?"

The boy sighs.

"It was just this guy asking me questions about Chase. If he lived here and—"

"Babe, we really really gotta go. It was probably just some real estate guy trying to buy up Brooklyn brownstones. You know how they do."

"Mmmhmm. Alright. Go on ahead to your little basketball game."

"Finally...sheesh," Devantay says.

He grabs the basketball and hurries out the gate.

Chase cradles Jenae's soft cheeks and tickles her nose with his. A calming breeze wraps them in a cocoon. He traces his finger from her temple, down her cheek to her bottom lip. He plucks it. Jenae grins.

"I love you," he says.

"I love you more," she replies.

As Chase walks toward the gate he feels a small *POP* on his backside. He turns.

"What? I can't smack my man's yummy yums?"

Chase smiles and shakes his head. Jenae nods for him to jog up to Devantay. The boy is already halfway down Henry Street heading towards Pineapple Street. Chase catches up.

"Dang, little man. You let Jenae punk you like that?" Chase says.

"Sorry yo, but she's good at that lawyer stuff."

"Yeah, yeah...Hey?" Chase says.

"What?"

"Race you to the court?"

"Uh huh," Devantay cheeses.

"Alright I'll count to three," Chase says. "One...two...." Chase tugs Devantay's shirt and bolts ahead before yelling...

"Threeee..."

"Hey, no fair," Devantay says. He sprints up the block after him.

———❦———

Rubber soles squeak against the blacktop. The orange ball bounces and echoes like a studio beat. Young men and old boys crash bodies, spit phlegm and talk smack. This is the basketball court. It's where a bruised ego bleeds more than a scraped knee. Especially with the pretty girls watching. And it's where a bare chested Chase, and a wide-eyed Devantay, dribble and swish in their 4th game of the afternoon. The Mister Softee ice cream truck rolls by with its super happy, nostalgic jingle.

"Swish. Like butter, baby boy. You might want some toast with that," a slender teenager brags to young Devantay.

The older boy has just stroked another jump shot from beyond the arc. Devantay grits his teeth with frustration. Three dribbles later the teen hits the same shot over Devantay's outstretched hand.

"Nothin' but net youngin'."

He brushes nonexistent dirt off of his wiry shoulders and raises two middle fingers in Devantay's direction. Devantay lowers his head and puckers his bottom lip. Chase calls time out.

"Aww, your fake Daddy gotta dry your tears now?" the adolescent tormentor says.

Chase glares at the youth before taking a knee at Devantay's side.

"Hey, don't be so down. The score is tied. We're not losing," Chase says.

"But I keep messing up. He's better than me."

His pupils get glassy.

"Hey. Look at me. No one is *better* than you. He's made a couple of shots. Big deal. And he's being cocky. That's called poor sportsmanship. And he's in for a rude awakening. People form opinions of you based on your attitude and your behavior. Bad attitude equals bad behavior which equals a bad life. You want to be like that?"

"No...but...but I'm not as good."

"Hey, all that matters is that you try."

"But I don't want you to be mad at me."

Chase pauses.

"Now, chin up. This game doesn't matter. You and I matter. I'm not your fake anything and I'll always be proud of you as long as you try your best."

Devantay's frown softens.

"Alright. Now come here. I got an idea."

Chase cups his hand to the child's ear and whispers. Devantay's face lights up. The next basket wins. Devantay inbounds the ball to Chase. Chase is a bit of a Cobble Hill Brooklyn basketball legend. The opposing team assumes he will be the hero. As Chase slices and dices through the defense, the tall teen who had been harassing Devantay all afternoon ignores the boy to go double team Chase. But as Chase jumps to shoot he instead fires a crosscourt pass to Devantay. The preteen catches the ball, cuts to the basket, and lays it in for the game winner.

"We won, we won, I did it, I did it," he shouts.

Chase sprints to the ecstatic child. He goes to high five him but Devantay pounces into his arms and squeezes instead. This is the first time Devantay has ever hugged Chase. The opposing team congratulates Devantay—except for his tormentor. The tall teen sulks under a sourgum tree. Devantay walks over to him and brushes his shoulders off. Chase smirks.

Mentor and mentee call it quits and head across the street towards the bodega. Chase cups Devantay's shoulder. The boy is on cloud nine. Chase thinks about the bigger picture. He recalls how he only decided to mentor Devantay because it enhanced his C.V. at Brooklyn University. Chase lacked anything that showed he was giving back to the community which is a part of the school's criteria for promotions. Chase's best friend, DJ Tanaka used to give free DJ lessons at Devantay's group home. He suggested Chase volunteer. The first conversation with the home's director, Amos James went like this:

```
"Devantay's father was a paranoid
schizophrenic with five suicide
attempts," Mr. James said.
"Five?" Chase said.
"Yes, but the sixth time was a charm.
Took a header off the George Washington
Bridge three years ago. Splat."
"What about Devantay's mother?"
"Oh, she was a real prize. Meth, crack,
heroin, petty crimes, prostitution. One
day a dealer said he could get her,
three times the amount of drugs he
normally sold her if she would bring
Devantay to a house to meet a man he
knew. One night, about a year ago, she
did just that. Somebody dropped dime to
the police. The mother went to jail and
since Devantay had no other family he
got put in the system.
"What about the man?"
```

"Don't know. They never caught the guy she sent him to. But Devantay refuses to discuss what happened that night."

They start to return to Chase's brownstone but as they pass the entrance to the A train, Chase stops.

"Hey?" he says.

"Yeah?"

"Yes, not yeah. Have you ever been to Times Square?"

"Times Square? Nope."

"Would you like to go?" Chase asks.

"Go? Like...now, go?"

"Sure. Why not? Train station is right here."

"Heck yeah."

"Let me just call Jenae and tell her just in case she was waiting around for us."

Chase autodials his ladylove and informs her of their new plans. He covers the mouthpiece and turns to Devantay.

"Jenae thinks we should shower before hopping on the train. Says we're probably sweaty and funky."

Devantay sniffs his underarms and shrugs. Chase returns to Jenae.

"I think we're just going to be the funk brothers for the rest of the day," he says.

Devantay giggles. Chance winces as he gets an earful.

"She said that's not funny. And I'm not setting a good example."

Devantay shrugs.

"Oh, come on babe. You don't mind my *funk* at other times," he snickers.

"What that mean Chase? Y'all being nasty again?"

"Shush, little man. You'll find out in a few years."

Chase says his goodbyes to Jenae and he and Devantay head underground down the musty Subway steps.

But in Chase's exuberance he hadn't noticed the large figure that trailed them from the court and was licking on an ice cream cone as he talked to Jenae. It's the fat man. He wipes his dripping fingers and dials his phone.

"Hey boss...it's me."

Why do you keep doing that?

"Oh right. Caller I.D. Sorry."

Forget it. What you got?

"I camped out in front of his place like you said. The chick he was getting freaky with at the school stayed all night."

The lawyer?

"Yeah."

You got her name?

"Yeah. Jenae Dixon."

Good. Find out where she works. Who her boss is. I want everything you can find on her.

"Something else. Chase is in some kind of big brother program at a group home. Mentors this kid named Devantay. I asked him a bunch of questions before Chase took him to play basketball."

Nice. Find out where the home is and who runs it. Basketball, huh? Hope they don't have any cheerleaders.

"Huh?"

Nothing. Just keep doing your job. It's almost time for Chase to get everything he deserves.

3 Up In The Cut

A maple leaf dances in the wind across the gritty playground. It bounces off the bridge of a first grader's nose. She giggles.

"You chilrun best stop throwing rocks at them squirrels," a rickety voice shouts from the park bench.

"Mind yo bi'ness old man," the little boy next to the girl says. He clutches a handful of his *squirrel popping* pebbles.

The elderly man shrivels his dried raisin cheeks and wriggles a decrepit finger.

"Boy, you best watch yo' mouth fo' I run tell yo' daddy."

"Ricky, we gonna get in trouble," the girl says.

"Kiyana, I'm in second grade now. You can do what you want in second grade. He a dumb ass old man. Daddy in jail. What he gonna do? Run his stink butt to the jail?"

"Haha, Ricky you said stink butt," Kiyana says.

"Come on. It's too cold out here anyways. Let's go back upstairs. Don't forget your scarf," he says.

Ricky takes his sister by the hand. They toddle past the monkey bars and swings into the sixteen story project tower. They run into the elevator. A nose pinching pool of piss ferments in the corner. Ricky reaches for the button on the panel.

"No, it's my turn. I want to," Kiyana protests.

Her brother shrugs and and backs away. Kiyana jumps up—just managing to smack button number eight. The elevator jolts a slow ascent. It lets out on the eighth floor. They pitter-patter down the cinder block hallway. Hip-Hop and merengue boom behind the apartment doors. The aroma of slow-cooked collard greens and

Mangú wriggle up their noses. Ricky raps his knuckles on a door at the end of the corridor.

"Quién?" a female voice calls answers.

"It's us," Kiyana echoes.

Metallic clicks, clacks are followed by a partial crack of the door. The two children push their way inside. They bump past a bony young man in a gold tank top and an oversized New York Yankees baseball cap. The textured handle of a nine millimeter Glock pistol, pokes from his waistband. Kiyana trips on his white sneakers as she scurries to the back of the apartment.

"Sorry, Hector," she says. The children run into a back bedroom.

"Morena. Cierra la fucking door already. And I told you about your sister's clumsy kids. I just bought these."

"I'm sorry Hector," Morena says.

The cinnamon brown Latina shuts the door and joins two bare breasted women at the kitchen table. It is cluttered with tiny brown cubes, wax paper wrappers, a currency counter, scales and money stacks. Hector texts constantly, but keeps a warden's eye on the raven haired women.

Ricky and Kiyana play in a room littered with dirty clothes, half-eaten sandwiches and condom wrappers. They join a pony-tailed girl in a Hello Kitty blouse, and a crying toddler in a lumpy diaper. His wailing has been ignored for two hours.

Discarded and neglected children will build worlds of wonder out of discarded and neglected things. Kiyana discovers a dozen bundles of cannabis. Her imagination turns them into green confetti. They find Hector's *Desert Eagle* handgun. This becomes the children's *magic hammer*. Hello Kitty girl mixes a bottle of vinegar with bags of white powder she found.

"Look, I made face paint. It will make us induh-vizble," she says.

"You mean *invisible* silly. You can't see me, you can't see me," Kiyana says, hiding her eyes behind tiny fingers.

They play with no concern from the adults until a loud *POP* shatters the window behind them. Seconds later the bedroom door bursts open. It's Hector. He's brandishing the glock. Morena is behind him.

"Yo, what the hell was that?" Hector says. His eyes zig-zag the room.

The toddler screams next to the shattered glass. The two girls huddle one another. Little Ricky clutches the Desert Eagle handgun. The gun's muzzle is obscured from Hector's vision by the bath towel little Ricky tied around his neck. It's his *superhero* cape.

As Hector gets his bearings he focuses on Kiyana.

"Wait, wait, espera, espera. What the hell is on y'alls faces?"

Hector grabs Kiyana by the back of her hair and wipes her cheek. He sniffs his fingers and tastes. His lips shrivel as if he licked a lemon. By reflex he glares at the closet to see an open shoebox.

"Hijo de puta [son of a bitch], y'all got in my stash? Get y'all asses over here," he demands. The girls shake their heads.

"Ven acá, ahora [Come here now]," he yells. He yanks Kiyana by the shoulder.

"Hector, por favor. No. Please don't," Morena pleads. Hector gun butts Morena in the jaw with his pistol. He yolks a terrified Kiyana by her throat and forces the little five-year old on her hands and knees. He shoves her face into the shoe box full of powder and spilled vinegar.

"You see this? Huh? Look at what you did. Smell it. Lick it. Look at it. Go ahead. Lick it you little whore."

Kiyana screams with terrified tears.

He paces back and forth pounding his temples with his fists.

"Hector they're just kids. They didn't—"

SMACK

Hector sends Morena into the wall with a backslap.

"Mierda [Shit]. You know how much money I lost in this mess? Do you, puta?"

Hector lunges at Morena. He climbs on top of her, wrings her neck, and presses the gun to her temple.

"Mira, please. Me voy a pagar, Me promiso [I promise to pay]."

"Bitch, you ain't got that kind of money."

He eyes Kiyana.

"But that one there? Yeah, I know someone who would pay large and quick for a night with that one."

He rolls from on top of Morena.

"Hector, no. Es mi sobrina. She's my niece."

Hector inches toward Kiyana with a sinister smile.

"So you like to play games? I'm going to bring you to somebody who knows lots of games for little putalitas like you."

Just as Hector reaches for Kiyana's arm…

POP POP

And his arm goes limp. His pistol drops. His knees buckle. And he collapses. Everyone is silent. Hector stops moving. A stream of red seeps from the smoking hole in his head. It collects at Kiyana's toes. The camera cuts to Ricky. At the end of his outstretched arms is the Desert Eagle handgun. The camera moves in tight.

"No one touches my sister."

The screen fades to black. Movie credits scroll up:

Brooklyn Fade Productions

in association with

Club Magma Enterprises

presents

Save The Children
A Dramatic Documentary
Directed by Kit Jude

Featuring
Javier Ramirez as *Hector*
Odalys Peña as *Morena*
Mustafa Olean as *Ricky*
Kiyana Bettenfield as *Kiyana*
Selena Ortiz as *Hello Kitty Girl*
Quentin Traylor as *the Toddler*
Tiffany Brown as *Drug Money Girl 1*
Demaris Lester-Van Sicklen as *Drug Money Girl 2*
and
Abdul-Haqq Salaam as *The Old Man on the Bench*

"Lights, please," someone says.

The packed bar/lounge applauds with a crescendo of hoots and hollers from the smartly dressed film buffs. Leaning on the bar stool in chocolate tweed slacks and a purple cardigan is the dapper Chase Archibald. Snaking her forearm under his bicep is Jenae. Her backless, plum evening dress hugs her soda bottle hips. She raises her mojito to her lips, slides the mint leaf to the side and savors a sip. Chase waits for her to swallow before swooping in with a surprise open mouth kiss. He sucks her tongue like a popsicle. It makes her back arch.

"Mmmm, tasty," Chase says.

Their eyes hug.

As the applause subsides as a middle aged man in a scruffy salt and pepper beard grabs the microphone.

"That was incredible wasn't it? We here at the *Dabka Lounge* are so proud to once again host the County of Kings Indie Film Fest."

"Hell to the yeah," a female voice screams.

"Okay, I want what she's drinking," he says.

The crowd laughs.

"And with the generous sponsorship of Club Magma owner Narcisse Marchant—thanks Narcisse [a tall slender man lifts his glass in the back]—we are so proud to bring films like these to the greatest city in the world...and the greatest borough, right?"

The crowd responds with the hip-hop chant of "*Broooklyn... Broooklyn.*"

Jenae brings her lips to Chase's ear.

"The rest of the evening is just artsy networking. Follow me, I have a surprise for you."

Jenae takes Chase by the hand. He thinks they're about to exit the bar. Instead they squeeze through artists, actors and film lovers toward a dark spiral staircase. At the bottom landing Jenae hands the bouncer two hologram VIP passes. He unhooks the velvet rope. They tip-toe into a discreet restaurant. Instead of tables there are seven pods separated by bamboo privacy panels. A model-thin man with a Valentino mustache greets them. He seats them on embroidered floor cushions. Jenae grabs one of the leather wrapped menus from between the flickering tea candles in the center.

"Can I get you two started with drinks? Or, if you already know what you would like I can put that in now?"

They peruse the menu arm-in-arm. Chase orders a glass of Chateau de Oupia Rosé for her and an Arnold Palmer iced tea for himself. They choose an appetizer of hummus, drizzled in Canaan Fair Trade brand olive oil, and order two grilled lamb and saffron rice house specials. The server nods and exits.

"You're smiling," Jenae says.

"You make me smile," he replies.

They cuddle in the dark amber light, surrounded by red and burgundy walls. A groovy jazz mix streams from the speakers above. Chase rests his lips on her forehead. He draws figure eights on the back of her wrist. She purrs.

"So what did you think of my friend Kit's film?" she asks.

The server returns with their drinks.

"Think? More like *felt*. It was so powerful. It reminded me of Devantay. And my own childhood," he says.

Jenae lifts her left eyebrow. She has tried on several occasions to get Chase to discuss his past. But Chase has always been elusive.

"In what way?" she asks.

His eyes trail.

"Come on honey. Tell me."

Chase fidgets. Jenae soothes his palms and coos her eyes. He melts.

"Well…not so much the drugs and violence thing. That was more Devantay's reality. But it was the lack of concern for children and how they seemed to just be an interruption in another man's life. And Hector was very controlling. No love at all. Like my father."

"You know babe, you never talk about your Dad."

"As she keeps reminding me," he says to himself.

"Which I shouldn't have to do, Mister Secretive."

"Fair point, fair point. Well, for one he was never *Dad*. Just, Pa. Stern. Standoffish. Cold. Even my mother called him Mister Archibald. Not honey, not even Bern—*cough cough* [Chase takes a sip] —sorry not even by his name…Vincent. Just, Mister Archibald."

Jenae's face turns quizzical.

"Hmm, that's kind of different," she says.

"Yeah I know, calling your husband by his last name right?" Chase says.

"Not just that. You always said you grew up in Boston, right?" Chase nods.

"But you just referred to your Dad as Pa, and your mother used to call him Mister Archibald. When I did my Masters thesis on *Family and Culture in the American South,* I found that what you just described —people using Pa for Dad and husbands and wives calling each other by their surnames—is an old southern thing. Never done up north. Odd."

Their food arrives. Chase shoves a wedge of pita and hummus in his mouth. A busy tongue helps to hide his sudden nervousness.

"Well, at any rate. I wish they were still alive," Jenae says.

"Yeah, well you know I don't like to talk about the accident that killed them," he says.

Jenae takes a sip of her rosé.

"I understand. So, tell me more about your funky trip to Times Square with Devantay."

Chase gives a lights laugh.

"We had a great time. Seeing Devantay so happy? Watching him experience the city as tourist? It made me feel good. But he did say something strange."

Jenae swallows a fork full of lamb and rice and nods for him to continue.

"On the subway ride back he asked me how I felt about you...whether I was in love."

"Oh really?...Hmmm, so how didst thou answer?"

She bites down on a stalk of asparagus with a pronounced *CRUNCH.*

Chase gets the obvious hint.

"Well, I saideth. Or is it sayith? You know, I don't even know the grammatically correct—

"Boy, just answer the question!"

"Okay, okay. I said that I was in unbreakable, rock solid love with you." He plants a kiss on her lips while her mouth is still full of food and won't let go.

"Mmph, Mmph. Stop you crazy man…you're gonna make me choke," she says between coughs and giggles.

"Sometimes you like when I make you choke," he says, and squeezes her exposed knee. She smacks it away.

"Finish the story frisky Freddy."

"So, here's the interesting part. He said…'Oh, so that means you're going to hurt her.'"

Jenae holds her fork mid-air and stares at Chase.

"Yeah babe, I had that look too," he says.

"So, what did you say then?"

"I said, 'Why would you say something like that?'And babe… without hesitation as if it were an encyclopedic fact he says…'Because when you love someone they hurt you. They will always hurt you. And then they'll leave."

"Wow, to be so young and so jaded," she says.

Chase and Jenae continue their dinner conversation. After forty-five minutes the waiter clears the table, takes their dessert orders, and returns to the kitchen.

Chase spiderwebs his fingers between Jenae's.

"I'm proud to be Jenae Monique Dixon's man," he says.

The statement makes Jenae's eyes pinch. Her cheeks dimple.

"Well, that sure came out of nowhere…But me likes."

"Come here," he says.

He puckers his lips onto hers and mops her soft palate with his moist tongue. She breathes heavily through her nostrils. The server returns with two bowls of sweet and spicy mango and dark chocolate gelato.

"Yoo hoo," he says, and places the desserts on the center console.

Their lips pull apart like string cheese. She snuggles into his neck. Her feathery, natural curls tickle his top lip. Shea and Argan oils slither up his nostrils. Chase dips the silver spoon in one of the bowls and scoops a peak of sweet gelato.

"Open up," he commands.

She cracks her mouth halfway.

"More," he demands.

She smiles and opens wider.

"I said more."

"Babe, I can't op—"

He pries her jaws open to their fullest with his thumb and index finger and plops a drop of the tangy goodness on her tongue.

"Mmm" she moans with a smile. "Wow. That chocolate and mango mix is dope...and is that cayenne they added?" she says.

"Let me see," he says.

Instead of taking a scoop for himself he dives into her mouth. His tongue slaps inside her cheeks with fury. Their lips smack. Their breaths snort. He savors the infusion of warm chocolate, bold mango and spice inside her mouth. He starts to break away.

"Uh, uh."

She grabs the back of his head and keeps their lips merged.

Chase leans Jenae flat onto the satin cushion. The tall bamboo shields them from onlookers. He spoons another decadent dollop but as he brings it to her lips it clops in the cleft of her cleavage.

"Oops," he smirks.

"Well...clean up your mess," she replies.

Chase reaches for the linen napkin.

"Uh, uh. *You* clean up your mess," she says.

Jenae cups his bald head and guides him to the juicy, ice-creaminess between her breasts. He sucks her clean. They rinse and repeat—losing themselves in a sensual foodie world. Chase claws her hair and pulls it back. Her exposed neck is a vampire's candy. He bites and sucks from her jugular to her collarbone and then inches her skirt up.

"Oh babe wait…wait what are you—?" Chase slides his hand inside her thigh and pricks the lace edge of her thoroughly moist panty to the side. A sticky honey coats his index and middle finger as he mimics the action of a tongue between a lover's hot cheeks. She moans with a shiver.

"Ding dong," the waiter says.

Chase bounces up.

"Oh, uh…um…uh."

The server puts his hand on his hip and waves his hand.

"Honey, please. These booths are an architectural aphrodisiac. I got stories for days. Anyway, I'd love to just make myself a busy little worker bee and buzz off but we're closing for the night. Sorry."

He places a small tray with two mints beside the empty bowls.

"Okay, you can bring the check," Chase says.

"Check? Child please. Miss thing handled her business when she made the reservation. Including the tip."

"Babe?" Chase says.

"My treat," she winks.

The waiter walks back towards the kitchen.

"You amaze me. You're just phenomenal."

"Phenomenal woman. Like Maya Angelou said."

Jenae sits up and straightens her attire.

"Oh, excuse me," she says to the waiter, halfway down the hall.

"Yes ma'am?"

"Can you pack a pint of that there gelato in a bag with some ice?" Jenae says.

"Sure thing. And by the way it's on the house," he says with a wink.

"Hope you're still hungry Mister Archibald," Jenae says.

"Only for a sweet, creamy bowl of Ms. Dixon."

While they wait for their lovers treat, unbeknownst to them, the fat man has been hunkered in the booth next to them all evening. The server returns with Chase and Jenae's dessert. He keeps a hawk eye on the sexy couple as they exit up the steps before turning his attention to the fat man.

"Here you go." He he hands him a computer printout. It contains Jenae's credit card information, employer address, and social media profile information. These are details that the exclusive club—with its six month waiting list—requires of all VIP guests. The fat man snaps a photo of the printout with his phone and slips the server five hundred dollars.

"Pleasure doing business with you," the waiter says.

4 Read The Memo

❧

Eighty-five acres, six piers, and a stunning East River view of Manhattan. Brooklyn Bridge Park is a rainbow coalition of rollerbladers, frisbee tossers and chatty hip-hop lovers. That latter has been milling about from the earlier outdoor DJ battle. Perched on the top rung of a wooden bench is Chase. He suffers through the latest, *they be hatin' on me,* rant from his best friend Tanaka Hirohito. The five foot three inch, 3rd generation Japanese-American has just finished competing in the Rebirth of Slick DJ Battle. Tanaka is an excitable fellow and a proud conspiracy theorist. And he's just been *robbed* of first place at the battle. Chase endures Tanaka's diatribe of outrage with elbows on knees and palms mashed in his cheeks.

"Chase? Chase, are you listening?"

"Huh? Yeah. Dude, I'm looking right at you."

"So why I had to ask you twice? Come on, don't try to play me out like that, son," he says.

"I'm listening Naka, sheesh," Chase says.

"Hmph. Anyway…so you saw what I did next right? I hit that backspin and then I froze. I made the crowd wait for like ten seconds. That's called a dramatic pause." Tanaka stops moving.

"Naka, you don't have to *actually* pause to make your point."

"And then…BAM, I dropped Brand Nubian's *Slow Down* out of like nowhere. Sickness son-son. Sick-Ness right? Wasn't that sick?"

"Yes. Very diseased," Chase says.

"Haha, very cute Professor Archibald. The point is I was robbed. See how they do a brother?"

Throngs of attendees file past. A gangly man, with a dark cauliflower beard and butt length dreadlocks recognizes Tanaka from the competition.

"Eh, wagwan. You dat DJ?" he says in a Jamaican accent.

"That's right yo. Big up one time my brother," Tanaka replies. He gives the man a hand clasp and an exaggerated *brohug*.

"Yuh set was wicked bredren, wicked meh say. Nuff respeck." The man closes his eyes with a chest bow and continues up the pedestrian path to Joralemon Street.

"Aha. You see that, Chase? You see that right there?"

Why did his cray-cray just get validated? Chase mumbles into his palms.

"Hey. I heard that. Keep drinking your haterade."

"Listen, if you're done with your manifesto, I wanted to run something by you. I've been thinking about—"

"Wait. Chase? Is...Is that?" Tanaka squints towards the pier. "Yup, that's her. Yo Lydia...Lydia. Yo, Yo Lydia."

He wiper-blades his arm to get the attention of a copper haired woman with Taino rope braids. She struggles with a heavy box of supplies while also shouldering a stuffed knapsack.

"Míra. Míra Lydia. Lydia. I know hear me. I know you see me mama. I got something to say to you," he says.

"Tanaka don't start," Chase says. "Lydia didn't have anything to do with you losing."

"Hey, I didn't lose. I was *robbed* R-O-B—"

"Oh no, not the spelling thing," Chase says.

The Nuyorican approaches with a scowl. She rolls her eyes and interrupts Tanaka before he can begin.

"Number one, thanks for being such a gentleman and helping a sister with all this shit. Number two, don't give me none of your diva DJ attitude. Every time you lose at one of my shows you gotta stress me out with your complaints. Boo-Boo you lost. L-O-S-T, lost," she says.

Chase snickers.

"Oh, so *she* can spell shit?" he says to Chase. "That's okay Lydia. The people gave me my props."

"What's he yapping about Chase?" she says.

"Somebody gave him a *light* compliment and now he's Grandmaster Flash."

"*One* represents the thousands my brother. I was robbed and Lydia knows it."

"The crowd makes the decision honey, not me. I still love you though. Te quiero papi. *Mwah.*" She squeezes Tanaka's cheeks into a pucker and smooches the air before heading off.

Chase shakes his head.

"She knew I won. You peeped that right? Hey, you peeped that right?"

"Oh yeah. I double and triple peeped."

"It was that damn hipster crowd. Once I started mixing the conscious music everything changed. A Tribe Called Quest, Latifah, Brand Nu…. They wanted that mush mouth, R2D2 beep scuuurr shit the other dude was playing. Damn interloper."

Chase chortles.

"Interloper? Why? 'Cause he was a white dude?"

"Don't patronize me."

"Bro you sound like Spike Lee complaining about gentrification in Brooklyn. I should crown you the Japanese Spike Lee. Just make sure you do the right thing? Haha get it? Do the right thing?"

"Crack jokes if you want to. Meanwhile, my people being squeezed out by these hipsters."

"Your people?"

"We all one blood. Stop sticking up for the capitalist, elitist, racially dismissive agenda of the money grubbing corporate oligarchs."

Chase opens his palm like a book and flicks his fingers.

"Chase, what the hell are you doing?"

"I'm looking up all those big words you just used."

"Oh you're a real comedian. Hardee Har Har. But I know why you're so desensitized to the situation."

"Situation? Dude there is no *situation*. You lost a DJ battle. Does this look like Selma or Ferguson to you? Pull your panties up. Stop crying."

"I'm not crying. But you got soft 'cause that redhead stole your righteousness."

"Oh no not this again. No Tanaka. I am not dealing with you and your Andrea fetish. Whenever you're losing an argument with me you have to bring her up. We dated for a few years when I moved to the city. That was seven years ago."

"Two words…the bitch is bad."

"Tanaka that's an entire sentence."

"Whatever. Andrea's a manipulator *and* she's crazy. And the fact that y'all remained friends after y'all broke up is totally wack. You lucky Jenae don't know Andrea's your ex. What woman is going to let you be friends with a chick you used to crush."

"First, that's crude. Second, no one *let's* me do anything. Jenae and I have a solid and secure relationship. She knows she has nothing to worry about with me."

"Really? So why haven't you told Jenae that you and Andrea used to smash huh? I mean the two of y'all so *safe* and *secure* and shit right?"

"It just never came up in casual conversation, okay?"

"Casual conversation? Brother is you for real?"

"Look, forget this ridiculous conversation. I want to ask you something. I've been thinking about my life and—"

Chase feels a poke on his elbow. A young boy has rolled up to the park bench on a scooter. He appears to be no more than seven. Chase hops off the park bench and kneels to greet him at eye level.

"Hey, young man. Are you okay? You lost?"

"Here." The boy shoves a white envelope under Chase's nose.

"Uh, okay. So what is this?" Chase asks.

"Fuck I know?" he says.

Chase frowns.

"Okay, profanity aside. Why are you handing this to me?"

"Yeah, and who are you anyway?" Tanaka says to the boy.

"Ain't nunna your business who I is," the boy snaps.

"What you say?" Tanaka says.

"It's who I am not is. Now, what is this?" Chase says.

"I said I don't know."

"Little punk. You better fix that attitude," Tanaka points.

"The man said he give me five bucks if I hand this envelope to the tall guy sitting on the bench in front of the crazy acting Chinese nigga."

"The what? What kind of racist ass—? Number one, I'm not even Chinese. Second, I—"

"Naka, not now," Chase says.

Chase surveys the park for the man the child mentioned.

"Where at?" he says to the boy.

"Uh-uh." The boy shakes his head. "I ain't no snitch."

Chase grabs the boy by the shoulders.

"Boy, if you don't show me who gave this to you I'm going let my crazy Asian friend whoop your little bad behind."

The child fires his finger at the parking lot. Chase only sees families, teens and a group of soccer players. The child shrugs.

"They was standing there just a minute ago."

"They? What did *they* look like?"

"Uh, I don't know. One was tall as you. He was wearing a suit. The other guy was really big though. And fat. Like Juggernaut from the X-Men. You know the X-Men?"

Chase clenches his fist and searches the lot with his eyes. But no luck.

"Ain't you gonna open it? I'll tell them what you said for another five bucks."

Tanaka's face turns foul.

"You don't even know where they are. Get on outta here you little hustler."

The little boy scrunches his face and sticks out his tongue. He hops on the hover board and whizzes toward the playground.

Chase pokes his finger in the flap and tears it open. He removes a tuft of paper. His eyes pop.

"Whoa. Dude. Your face. You okay? What does it say? Hey, if we gotta handle some business you say the word. You know your boy is nice with the hands."

Tanaka starts shadow boxing.

Chase remains petrified but his hand trembles.

"Bro, what does it say? Let me see."

Chase swallows a lump in his throat. He reads the letters over and over—not because the words are many—but because the words are so few. They appear as if cut and glued from a magazine. The note reads:

We. FOUNd. YOU.

Chase squeezes his bald head and bites his lips.
"Chase you're scaring me, man. What does it say?"
He crumples the note before responding and says...
"It says...it says I have a problem."

❧

HUH, PAT PAT...HUH, PAT PAT...HUH, PAT PAT
He sucks in the South Street Seaport air through cavernous
nostrils. His nightly jaunts have crept into the day. As he approaches
the pedestrian crosswalk under the FDR drive, he jogs in place. His
eyes bounce from lost tourist, to a mother and a carriage, to a
Halloween shopper. A taxi beeps from behind a box truck. He waits
for the light to change.
"Buff Puff? Buff Puff is that you?"
The words drift from a crouched woman curled in a soiled
comforter. By her toe is a soda cup. Two strangers converse in a
foreign tongue. They squat and rattle two quarters in her till before
moving on.
"It is you Buff Puff. Look at you snorting like a brahma bull. I
got something better for you to snort up under this here blanket
though," she says, and lifts the cover.
Chase ignores the obscene flirtation. Her face softens as she sees
her reflection in his glassy eyes.

"Aww, Buff Puff. Look at them eyes. What's wrong baby?" she says.

"Wrong? Miss Pat, what makes you think—"

"Boy, don't play with me. I'm old, not stupid."

Chase's mind has been in flux for a week. Ever since that day with Tanaka in the park. Perhaps a gentle ear…any ear, would help soothe his troubled mind.

"Miss Pat I—"

"Wait boy. I can't hear for a goddamn. All this city noise. Noise, noise, noise. Ugh. Help me up. We can go yonder, by the dock."

She clutches her change cup while steadying herself on his shoulder. The dirty cover drops to the grimy asphalt. Chase carries it for her. Her port-o-potty odor stings his eyes and burns his nostrils. As they stroll to the pier, Chase relates what occurred at Brooklyn Bridge Park. He tells her of Tanaka and the DJ battle…but when he gets to the cryptic note Miss Pat blurts:

"Aha. I knew there was something all secret-secret about you. I smelled secret all over you. Secret Buff Puff. Secret. Secret. Secret," she claps.

Chase indulges her schizophrenic moment before continuing.

"Miss Pat, I don't know what to do. I can't have this kind of drama in my life right now."

"Do you know what this note thing is all about?" she says.

"No. I don't. Well…maybe it has to do with this thing in my past…you know what, never mind it's nothing."

"I been around a long time Buff Puff. You hiding *something*."

Chase's gaze drifts to the rocky ripples of the East River. "I just don't know what to do Miss Pat."

"Do? Boy, man up. Live your damn life that's what you do. All you can do." Her thoughts in a different but related direction. "Let me tell you something 'bout me. You know Radio City Hall right?"

Chase nods.

"Well, I was a Rockette. In the eighties. Didn't know that did you? Mmmhmm. You shoulda seen me. I had all the fellers lusting after me. That man could be as black as a thousand midnights or as white as death. Didn't matter none. 'Cause when my smooth, long, luscious legs kicked up a storm? Ooh wee them boys practically wet themselves. And I don't mean the pee-pee kind neither."

Chase winces.

"They sure wanted some of Miss Patty McShane. I ain't have to worry 'bout no money or nothing. Men love spending money on pretty girls. Especially ugly men. Makes them feel important. Reckon 'cause they so damn ugly. If God don't give you beauty for free, the devil will sell you a taste for a fee. I was something special in my day. But everything gets old eventually. And people just…well they just throw the old things away."

She glazes at the Queens skyline from the dock.

"But I have plans, Miss Pat. This thing I'm dealing with—"

"What thing?" she growls back. "Your past?"

Chase doesn't respond.

"No matter. I can already tell it's about your past. You just gotta live your life. That's what I was getting at. A random scrap of paper got you all emotional like you some woman caught up in her feelings? That ain't cute, Buff Puff. Tain't cute at all. Did anybody tell you what they want?"

Chase shakes his head no.

"Show up at your job?"

Chase shakes again.

"Boy, go live your life. You stressin' for nothin'. Now, unless you 'bout to finally give Miss Pat some lovin', you go on and get."

Chase's eyes widen. He grabs Miss Pat and hugs her. He ignores the dirt and stench of harsh life on the street. His embrace is warm and non-judgmental. But for all her dirty talk, her arms stiffen at her hips. How long has it been since a man held her? How long since she felt the comfort of human touch?

"All-all right now. Don't you go startin' somethin' you can't finish."

She jerks away.

Chase reaches into his back pocket and pulls out a wad of twenty dollar bills. Her pride fly-swats it away. She grabs her blanket and shuffles back to her corner. Chase notices that she has forgotten her change cup. He bundles the money she refused to accept inside.

"Miss Pat, hey Miss Pat you forgot this," he says.

"Gimme that," she snatches.

Chase smiles and strolls back to the pier. He leans on the dock rail. The waves slap the barnacles on the wood pilings. A renewed sense of purpose soaks into his heart. Miss Pat's perspective gives *him* perspective. He removes a business card from his front pocket and thumbs his finger over the fancy raised lettering:

Jannsen Jewelers

958 West 47th Street Suite 3
New York, NY 10036
212.555.1971
"Prove to her you mean forever,

with a diamond that says…right now"

Chase beams to the horizon. But his joy will be short-lived. The note was a calling card. And a blast from the past is about to come calling.

5 Allow Me To Reintroduce Myself

Brooklyn University. Polka dot bow ties, and skinny jeans mingle with thrift store sweats and Sikh turbans. But they don't linger. Today starts the weekend. At the base of the lecture hall Chase answers a question from the last to file out, Robbie Jankovic. The young man is now the most attentive student in class.

"Although it isn't a work of fiction, Claude Brown's gritty storytelling will help you to write better. Good writers are good readers," Chase says.

"Thank you professor. I'll read *Manchild in the Promised Land* over the holiday break. Have a Happy Thanksgiving," Robbie says.

Chase feels inside his leather satchel for his earbuds. Tonight is Hip-Hop karaoke at Brooklyn Bowl, a converted warehouse that is now a hot club and bowling alley. Jenae and her sister Shauntelle rocked the crowd last month with *Ladies First* by Queen Latifah and Monie Love. That gave them bragging rights over Tanaka and Chase who stunk up the joint with a weak rendition of *What's The Scenario?* Tanaka, of course, felt that the crowd was gender biased and being sympathetic to *those females*. He also voiced his opinion that Chase's weak rhyming skills contributed to their defeat. Chase wants karaoke redemption and the opportunity to rub Shauntelle's face in defeat. Jenae's strong-willed sister is someone Chase has never quite cared for. The feeling is mutual.

Robbie exits the lecture hall. Just as the metal door is about to shut, a meat slab of a hand juts inside. It creaks the door back open.

Two figures emerge at the top step. A throat clears.

Chase lifts his gaze. His jaw drops. Two men. One he has never seen before. He has the girth of a Sumo wrestler in a claustrophobic blue suit. It's the fat man. Next to this behemoth is a gentleman in a grey pinstriped black suit, pressed shirt and gold tie. It is *he* that is the jaw dropper. He reads aloud from a tablet computer in his palm.

"I recommend Professor Archibald highly," he says—mimicking the voice of a perky freshman. "He's tough, but fair. Plus he's like such a hunk. O-M-G can I like really say that? Oh well, already did." He eyeballs Chase. "I see you still got these little cottontails running after you, huh bruh?"

Chase wrings the handle on his briefcase with such force, it sounds as if he's scraping the skin from his palms. The two men descend the steps. The slimmer one drops the tablet in front of Chase. The screen reveals Chase's faculty bio, class schedule and student reviews.

"You look surprised. Didn't you get my little note in the park?"

Chase burns a cold stare.

"Speechless? What's with the ice grill? You're going to make Man-Man think we're not friends."

"We're *not* friends, Eugene," Chase says.

"It speaks! But I don't know if I like how he said it. There was no...warmth. Did you feel any warmth?"

Man-Man shakes his head.

"Goodbye Eugene," Chase says. He walks to the steps.

Eugene extends an arm to block him.

"Not so fast, Sparky. I'm really interested in this professor scam of yours."

"Scam?"

Chase brushes Eugene's arm away.

Eugene jumps into his path again.

"I mean with reviews like these, I should become a so-called *professor* too. Maybe you could introduce me to this hot little bunny rabbit with the review. I hope she's not some blonde, blue-eyed, snowflake thought. We all know how well that worked out for you last time huh? Hahahaha."

"I don't have time for your little mind games, Eugene. Now move."

He stomps towards the first level of the staircase. Eugene's burly sidekick steps into Chase's path. He bounces off of him like a cue ball. And at six foot three, Chase isn't used to having to look *up* to someone.

"Let me give you two a more formal introduction. Chase—that's the name you're using right? Chase meet Man-Man. Man-Man, meet Chase. I really need to get used to this Professor Archibald thing of yours."

Chase sizes Man-Man up.

"I know what you're thinking. Can I take these dudes? You might have a shot with me. On one of my bad days. But this big boy here? Know why we call him Man-Man? 'Cause he's like two big ass mofos in one. Look at him. He ain't a man...he's a *man*-man. So you might wanna back your punk ass up."

Chase surveys the situation and realizes the wiser move is to play it cool and see what Eugene really wants.

"Go up the steps and watch the door," Eugene says to Man-Man. "Chase you have a seat."

Chase remains standing.

"That wasn't a request," Eugene says.

Chase hesitates before pulling down the folding seat in the front row.

"Chase Archibald? Oh my. That sounds so gangsta, ooooh," Eugene trembles his fingers in Chase's face.

"I am not interested in your silly jokes. Just say what you came here for and bounce."

Eugene sucks his teeth and wags a disapproving finger.

"See now…that right there. That's what I always hated about you. Always acting like an arrogant be-yatch. You on easy street far as I can see. Got you a million dollar brownstone. Primetime college gig. Hell, you even got you a big booty lawyer chick. Smart *and* sexy. Shit. Maybe we should pay her sweet little onion ass a visit too. Man-Man, you said she lives in Fort Greene right?"

Chase snaps. He jumps up and chokes Eugene by his necktie. Hot spit flies from Chase's gums as he shouts into his tormentor's irises.

"You wanna keep playing games with me? Huh? You been stalking me? Following my lady?"

Eugene's eyes bulge and his throat gurgles.

Responding to the commotion, Man-Man thuds his way down the steps. Eugene holds up his palm.

"Okay, okay. I'll give you a pass on your emotions this one time. Talking about a man's chick would set anybody off. Now stop spilling your feelings in the air. Let go."

Chase won't release.

"You really don't want the alternative bruh." Eugene glances at Man-Man.

Chase grinds his jaw before he loosens his grip.

"So, you've been stalking me? You and—," Chase pauses as he makes the connection between Man-Man and the *man* Devantay mentioned he saw on the stoop.

"Stalking is such a creepy word. We've simply taken an interest in your whereabouts."

Man-Man returns to guarding the door.

"What do you want, Eugene?"

"Want? Not much. A simple task."

"Task? I'm not doing anything for you. You know what? We're done here," Chase grabs his bag to leave. Eugene stiff-arms him.

"Sit your black ass down. This ain't no damn request. You done forgot where you came from, playboy? You done forgot who you owe this fake ass life of your too? You know how he handles ungrateful muhfuckas, right?"

Chase's heart pounds.

"Yeah, I know that look. So since I have your attention...here's the deal, cupcake. We got this thing going. We got a dude in A-T-L. We got another in Houston, L.A., the Chi. But the real opportunity is right here in New York. New York can do what all the other cities can do combined."

"What are you squawking about Eugene?"

Eugene parks himself in the seat next to Chase and leans into his shoulder.

"This city is full of single women right? I'm talking quality chicks. Not a bunch of ratchet hoes. Bitches with they own money, education, they do all that travel around bucket list shit. They on that Beyoncé, Miss Independent bullshit. But for whatever reason...they don't have no kids. No man. And no viable prospects. But peep this... they want one...not the dude. They want the kid *without* the dude, feel me? So that's where you come in, playboy. You gonna be that dude."

Chase sits up in his chair. He squints into Eugene's eyes as if he's searching.

"Are you on that shit again?" Chase says.

"That what?...No, nigga. Goddamn, I gotta spell it out for you? You meet bitches. You lay pipe. We get paid. But you gotta make sure you bust off inside. That's the whole point. So, no condoms."

Chase stares at him with a blank face.

"Oh and then you just bounce. You ain't even gotta cuddle up and act like you care about their feelings and shit. Every man's dream."

Chase is speechless.

"You are a certified nutcase. I don't care if he sent you."

Chase gets up. Eugene pulls him down by his sleeve.

"Bitch, sit the fuck down. You think we forgot about you? You got set up real nice, *Chase*. Didn't you?"

"I built my own life."

"Oh really? With no help from him?"

"Goodbye Eugene."

Chase walks up the stairs. Before reaching the third step, a colossal claw engulfs his throat and squeezes. Chase grabs at the trunk sized forearm as it impales him. The giant's other palm slams against his chest and lifts him off the carpet. His arms flail about. Man-Man grins as his clamps paralyze Chase.

Eugene stands to the side, *literally* humming a tune. He unwraps a stick of Wrigley's gum and pops it in his mouth. He chomps on the sweet and sticky wad enjoying Chase choke with sadistic glee.

Chase struggles to free himself but even five days a week at the gym cannot budge the human tree trunk. His mouth foams at the corners. His eyes puff and the whites redden.

"Okay, ease up...don't want him to pass out. Sit him in the chair," Eugene says.

Man-Man drops Chase to the dirty carpet instead. Chase coughs and gasps. The buttons on his collar have popped to reveal Man-Man's sausage like, finger impressions on his neck.

"*Now* are you listening?" Eugene says.

Chase gives a meek, beta male acknowledgment as he massages his larynx.

"Good, back to the plan. So these chicks will already be lined up for you. Paying to get pregnant. But they know the baby daddy don't come with the deal. Which is cool 'cause all they want is that D. The full experience."

"What woman would—?"

"Shush I ain't done. They don't want any random joker. They want that smart, handsome, athletic, type. With a clean bill of health…you are clean right? Eh, of course you are. You was always a goody two shoes."

"All this drama because you want me to be a male prostitute?"

"A hoe? Nah, I thought this—I mean *we* thought this through. Prostitution is about paying for sex. This is about paying for that seed. That's why it ain't illegal. It's brilliant."

"Let me get this straight. I'm supposed to get paid to have sex with—"

"Impregnate," Eugene corrects.

"What's the damn difference?"

"Sperm, nigga, sperm. Da fuck? You're supposed to be a professor? When you pay for sex that's prostitution. But they're not paying for sex. They're paying for your sperm. The sex is simply how they get it."

"Simply? This is a criminal enterprise Eugene."

"No it isn't. I researched this shit. Europeans do this surrogate thing all the time. They fly to a poor country. Pay some third world farmer's daughter to insert a dude's sperm. She gets pregnant. Nine months later? Squat, drop, pop, swish, nothing but net. She gives the baby to the couple, family gets paid, and everybody's happy."

"If it's so legit and easy, you do it."

"Eh. I know my limitations. I'm a little rough around the edges. That works great when females are still young and dumb. But when they get older? They want a square, bitch-ass nigga like you."

"Fuck you, Eugene. I'm not doing this."

"You wouldn't have this cushy life if it wasn't for us. But hey…if you don't want to do it. Fine. Forget it about it."

"Forget about it?"

"Yeah, just forget it. I'll just tell everybody who you really are and what you did before you got here. I'll tell your lawyer chick and the firm she works for, your boss Dean Ganges—yeah I know her name, the group home your little sob story brat be at—the director is Mister James right? I'll tell *every* damn body about their lying ass golden child so-called Professor Chase Archibald. So you got two choices. What's it gonna be? Door number one, you keep on being Chase or door number two? Bye-bye job, bye-bye little boy, Bye-bye sexy bitch."

Chase takes a shallow breath. His palms are slimy. His throat the Sahara. He doesn't know what to do. *I need time to think…I have to stall him,* he says to himself.

"Even if I assume you're right about the legalities. Why don't these women just go to a fertility clinic?"

Just as Eugene is about to answer, Man-Man yells down.

"Yo boss. Somebody coming."

Chase buttons his shirt and tucks in his shirt tail. Man-Man comes bounding down the steps. The door opens. It's Dean Ganges.

"Oh," she says, startled. "I didn't know you were in a meeting Professor Archibald. Is that why you didn't make our six o'clock?"

"Oh, right. Dean Ganges, I'm so sorry. I for—"

Eugene interrupts.

"Dean Ganges is it?" He extends his arm, places her hand between his palms, and clasps as if she were a pearl in an oyster.

"Yes, I'm Dean Ganges." she says, raising her brow at his handshake.

"My apologies ma'am. My associate and I are old friends of the professor. We're visiting for the weekend and decided to surprise him. It's not his fault. He did mention to us earlier that he had to get to a meeting with a very lovely colleague. He didn't say how much of a chocolate goddess she was," Eugene says.

"Well, I doubt Professor Archibald referred to me as his lovely colleague. I am a chocolate goddess however," Dean Ganges smirks.

"Indeed," Eugene says.

"A goddess who can recognize a bullshit line when she hears one," she says with a smile that isn't a smile.

All three men stand in an awkward silence.

"Professor, we can just reschedule."

"Oh no, please. We can continue our conversation with Chase tomorrow. We'll be here a while," Eugene says, slapping his palm on Chase's shoulder. "In fact we can drop by tomorrow. You're on Henry Street right, Chase?"

Chase strains his facial muscles to prevent a frown.

"Good," Eugene says.

He and Man-Man traipse up the steps and exit the lecture hall.

Dean Ganges remains. Chase does his best to mask his emotions as they begin to discuss the first item on their agenda but Chase's mind is elsewhere. Perhaps sensing his discomfort she cuts the conversation short.

"Chase, let's continue this next week."

"Dean Ganges I'm sorry. I'm just not—"

"No worries. Next week."

She gives him a hug, a polite peck on the cheek, and leaves.

Chase slumps in the chair. He swallows the lump in his throat. He glances at the burnt orange rays of the setting sun. He wonders if it's a metaphor for his own sunny days that are about to darken.

6 Party Pooper

✦

Her intoxicating scent tickles his nose. A finger slinks across his chest. He is somewhere between dream and reality until velvety fingers stroke his inner thighs. They trigger a rise. His eyelids awaken with a yawn. He sits up on his elbows but she shoves him back to the mattress. She straddles him with healthy thighs as her ankles coil and lock underneath his calves. Her cocoa butter palms brace his pecs. And then she churns. She pops her back. And churns. And pops. And churns. It is as if her hips were juicing a lemon.

He pinches the chocolate pecan peaks of her buttery breasts. She loves when he dials them between his fingers.

"Ah-oh-ow," she says. They sting with pleasure.

They don't just love with passion. They have a passionate love.

"I love you so much baby," he says, between sloppy kisses.

"I love—mmm—uh huh—love you—mmm—too...birthday boy."

She starts licking and lapping her way down his stomach. She stops her journey before he wants her to. He fingers her wispy golden brown curls to guide her but she resists.

"Jenae," he whines.

"Hee, hee, hee. Payback," she says with a diabolical grin.

She doesn't continue to drive him insane much longer before she drops her jaw with a smile. Her warm, sweet lips engulf his throbbing, succulent—

BANG BANG BANG

"Yo, Chase."

BANG BANG BANG

"Yo, Chase. Wake up playa."

The bangs and yells come from outside his open bedroom window.

Jenae glares up at Chase.

"Ugh. Tanaka," Chase says with a sigh. He flops his back on the pillow.

"And you wonder why I don't like your bestie," Jenae says.

BANG BANG BANG

"Yo Chase. Your doorbell ain't working. Wake up playaaa."

"I know you're not crazy about him. But he's my best friend and he's a good dude, babe," Chase says.

"He has the timing of a two year old," she scoffs.

Chase rolls out of the bed. He accidentally pulls the sheet off with him. It exposes Jenae's derriere.

"Mmm, nice," he says.

"Too late now playaaa," she says, tossing up mock gang signs. "Go throw something on for your little boyfriend."

Chase scampers into the master bath and cups a few splashes of water onto his face. He grabs last night's blue jeans a long-sleeved tee. He heads downstairs and opens the door for Tanaka. Tanaka has an overstuffed paper bag in one arm. His overgrown mop of black hair obscures his eyes as he walks in.

"Yo, yo. Happy Birthday big bro," he says.

He shoves the bag in Chase's gut like a quarterback to a running back.

"Ooof—Okay, what's this?" Chase says, as he digs in the bag. "Bagels? You bought me a dozen bagels for my birthday?"

"That's a baker's dozen so there's actually thirteen in there. You got anything to drink?"

Chase follows Tanaka into the kitchen and sets the bag on the counter near two bottles of Fiji water.

"So, the big 3-0 is today, huh?"

Tanaka grabs a carton of orange juice from the fridge and starts chugging from the container.

"What took you so long to—GULP, GULP, AAAH—answer the door?"

Jenae walks in, in black leggings, and a periwinkle tunic.

"Oooh, never mind. I see what took you so long."

Jenae gives Tanaka a side-eye as she pours herself a glass of water.

"Hold up, I know you not up here drinking my juice out of the damn carton," she says.

"This is Chase's crib. I can't keep inventory on your shit versus his shit," he fires back.

"Yeah? How 'bout I inventory these size eight Reeboks up your tiny ass?"

"Come on Tanaka chill. You're my boy but this here is my boo," Chase says.

Jenae sticks her tongue out at Tanaka. She pats Chase on the tush and sniffs inside the paper bag. She removes a cinnamon raisin bagel.

"Hey, I bought those for Chase," Tanaka says.

"Boy, please. Make yourself useful and hand me the butter," she says.

Tanaka grits his teeth and slides her a stick of butter from the refrigerator.

"And whatever with that boo stuff. I met Chase first. Years ago. Your bagel stealing behind only been around for three years."

"And I'll still be here when your unemployed ass is gone."

"I *have* a job. I'm a self-employed DJ."

"Hah. That's a hoot."

She butters her bagel.

"Can you two not fight for once? It is my birthday remember?"

"Aight Chase, you right, you right. I'll be the bigger man."

"Hmph. You'll need a step stool for that," Jenae says, dangling half-a-bagel.

"Don't you have a spell to cast or something?" Tanaka says. "By the way, Chase. I need that flash drive I lent you."

"Flash drive? Oh yeah, the 90's hip-hop mix that you put together?"

"Yeah, that's the one."

"Okay, I'll get it. It's in my leather bag."

Chase walks into the living room.

"Good...I need it for your party tonight."

Chase's eyes pop. Jenae slams her glass on the marble counter top with such force, it's shocking that it doesn't break. She arches her eyebrows and clenches her fists. Contempt for Tanaka shoots from her pores. He gulps a throat full of orange juice with a goofy—*Oops*—on his face.

Jenae stomps over to him and stabs her finger just millimeters from his forehead.

"What part of my text message: Reminder...*surprise* thirtieth birthday celebration for Chase tonight at eight, did you *not* understand you moron?"

"Uh...um...uh."

"You had one job. *One*. Be the DJ. That's it. Tap a button on a computer. Spin a record. Frankly, it's the only thing you actually do a halfway decent job at...other than run your damn mouth."

Chase attempts to butt in.

"Honey. It's okay, I—"

"Did she just give me a compliment?" Tanaka says.

"I can't believe this. This was supposed to be a surprise. A surprise," she yells.

"Babe, babe chill. I knew already," Chase says.

Jenae stops mid-rant.

"What do you mean you knew?"

"Well, I wasn't going to spoil the surprise but one of your friends, I won't say who, but one of them forwarded the party invite to me. Obviously, by mistake."

"Hah, ha-ha-ha. So it was one of your friends Miss thangy, thang, thang," Tanaka says, with a victory shimmy shimmy dance.

"Oh, shut up," Jenae says.

Chase eyes the disappointment on Jenae's face. He wraps her in his arms and presses his forehead to hers.

"Baby, no one is more important to me than you," he says.

Tanaka clears his throat.

"You mean more to me than a hundred birthdays. You gave me the greatest surprise any man could ever ask for when you walked into my life."

"Oh gag me with a spoon. I'm going in the other room," Tanaka says.

"But it was supposed to be a surprise," she says, poking her bottom lip.

"Awww, come closer," he says.

"But I'm already close," she baby talks.

"Not this kind of close," he says.

Chase cradles her cheeks and kisses her frown…repeatedly.

"Mmm, you always know how to pull a woman from the ledge."

"Hey, I have to tell you a secret," he says.

"What's your secret?" she replies.

He presses his lips to her ear.

"I heard Chase loves Jenae," he whispers.

"Really? Wow. You what? I heard Jenae loves Chase more," she replies.

Tanaka rolls back into the kitchen from the living room. He has a wafer thin flash drive between his fingers.

"So is the show over now? I found the drive in your bag myself."

Chase nods once to acknowledge Tanaka but his smile remains on Jenae.

"Babe, you should probably get ready for Devantay now. I'm going upstairs to take a long, lonely shower," Jenae says with an obvious wink and heads upstairs.

She winks and heads up.

"So where you taking the little dude?" Tanaka says.

"The transit museum, downtown Brooklyn sooo…" Chase says.

He gives Tanaka the hitchhiker thumb sign.

"Alright, I get it. I got stuff to do anyway. I'll catch you later tonight at Andrea's," Tanaka says.

"Andrea's? Why would I be going to—? Oh. The party is at Andrea's," Chase says.

"You should know that. You said you got the party invite by mistake."

Chase doesn't respond.

"Oh snap…that wasn't true?"

"Cover your mouth, fool. Not so loud," Chase says. "I love my lady and you're my boy. I wasn't going to let you be the one to ruin her surprise with your motor mouth. I had to think quick. Now get on out of here. I have some unfinished business in a shower," Chase says.

He and Tanaka fist bump and brohug. Chase closes the door behind him and sprints up the steps. Moments later the misty sound of the shower mixes with the moans of love under a porcelain rain.

❧

DUMBO. The Brooklyn neighborhood of technology and creativity nestled under the Manhattan Bridge. Tonight Andrea Lisi has opened her cavernous $5900/month penthouse loft towards celebrating Chase's 30th. The commemoration boasts the city's top young creatives, academics and professionals on the come up— including a stock broker friend of Andrea's. Andrea's collection of anti-fascist pop art decorates the walls. Wine, wings…and more wine satiate the masses. And a chilled house mix from DJ Tanaka is on the ones and twos. This party is popping.

Andrea is a five eleven ginger with bright emerald eyes, alabaster cheeks and cayenne freckles. Her obsession with squats— and her Polish genes—give her thighs and rump a thickness that twists necks. But her romantic history with Chase is known only to Tanaka. At this moment she sits on a wooden stool twirling a gin and tonic. Chase and Jenae snuggle in the love seat across from her. Andrea's tongue tends to lose its filter when she's sipping on the sauce.

"Hold up. He *actually* said that? Like out loud?" Jenae asks.

"Yes, girlfriend. Not only did he say that. He leaned in, asked me how bad I wanted a university fellowship, and then whipped out his stubby, little—"

"Oh my God not his?" Jenae covers her cheeks.

"—his stubby, little hand and squeezed my thigh. Then he started rubbing my knee like a genie was going to pop out my panties and grant him three wishes."

Jenae explodes in laughter.

"You never told me Dean Whitaker did that to you," Chase says.

"Uh, 'cause you're my *friend* not my man. I don't tell you everything,"she says.

"Forget him, Andrea. What happened next? Oooh this is so scandalous."

"Well, I thought to myself. Hmm…how can I turn this to my advantage?"

"Figures," Chase mumbles.

Andrea cuts her eye.

"So, I distract with some of this low cut boob action. All up in his face right?"

"Uh huh, okay, okay," Jenae says.

"I sneak my phone out my Kate Spade clutch."

Jenae moves to the edge of her seat.

"I switch on my bimbo voice and say, Oh Daddy I love it when you talk dirty to me. Say it again, say it again….*then* I press record. Would you believe dumb ass repeated that shit?"

Jenae cackles.

"He went full pervert. Just telling on himself. How he's gonna lick this, suck that as long as I played nice with the teacher. If I didn't then my fellowship would be gone. Girl it was gross. But I got his sexually harassing ass."

"So, that's why Dean Whitaker retired all of a sudden. Is that also how you became an associate professor so fast?" Chase says.

"Let's just say a great job and these nice digs don't come cheap. I always make sure people get what's coming to them. Harass me or humiliate me and you're going to feel my wrath. Anyway, time for me to be a good hostess and make my rounds," Andrea says.

She scoots off the stool.

Jenae cocoons inside her man's embrace. She tilts her neck back and rolls her eyes up to his.

"I love you Professor Archibald."

He advances his lips to hers.

"I love you too Attorney Dixon."

They kiss a long, syrupy sweetness.

"Now hold that thought. Something I gotta do," Chase says.

He slides from under Jenae and walks to the DJ table.

"Excuse me. Everyone. Hello. Excuse me. Can I have your attention please?"

The room of over one hundred quiets down. Chase nods to Tanaka who proceeds to cue Sade's *Kiss of Life*. The British siren's mellow croon is a slow sip of warm cider. It sets the stage for what is to come.

"Well, as some of you know, I moved to the city seven years ago. A Boston kid in Yankees country," Chase says.

"Yeah, the Jeter and Mariano days," a man yells from the back.

"Exactly, Professor Scobee. But this city is nothing without the people who give it life. All of you. Like Tanaka my best friend. Dean Octavia Ganges my boss, my mentor, and the closest I've had to a mother since my parents died in a car accident ten years ago."

"That would be Diva Dean Octavia Ganges, Chase," she says.

Everyone laughs.

"But out of everyone, every woman, there has only been one who was *the* one. All others meant nothing to me."

Chase fixates on Jenae who is still seated across the room. She sits up…confused. But who Chase doesn't notice is Andrea. He arms are crossed and she wears a tight scowl. Her beautiful green pupils have turned the color of murky pickle juice. She mouths a silent— *What the fuck?*—to herself.

Chase paces to Jenae. The normally confident and commanding attorney shrivels in her chair. Her palms quake.

"Jenae. I know you put together my birthday celebration. But there's a more important milestone I want us to celebrate."

A hush, like a fast fog, engulfs the penthouse. Chase takes a knee. Tanaka comes from behind the DJ table and hands Chase a purple velvet box. Jenae's pupils glisten to a watery sheen. Andrea's eyes sting with a burning flame. The redhead fumes as she stomps into the bathroom unnoticed.

Jenae digs her right hand into the armrest. Chase takes her other palm and utters…

"Jenae Monique Dixon…will you marry me?"

Chase flips the box open. A platinum five carat, princess cut diamond ring shines into her gaze. Jenae's jaw bobs up and down like a swimmer in a pool of trouble. Her chestnut cheeks flush red with excitement. She beams and jumps into Chase's arms. She starts to kiss him all over.

"So does that mean yes?" he says.

"YES! YES! YES!" she shrieks.

The crowd roars. Chase slips the ring onto her slim finger. A throng of women rush to her as a mob of men congratulate Chase. Tanaka cues the old McFadden and Whitehead song, *Ain't No Stoppin' Us Now.*

The room is a joyful noise. A joyful noise with one whimpering soul…Andrea. She has watched what has just transpired through the crack of the bathroom door. She pops out. Chase's surprise announcement has her seething with bitterness.

"Out of *every* woman there's been just one? All others meant nothing? Nothing he says," Andrea grumbles.

"Oh, thank God you're out. I've been holding it in. Please say you're done now?" Professor Scobee says, squeezing his crotch like a little girl who needs to tinkle.

"Yeah, yeah," Andrea grunts. He bolts into the toilet.

A bubble of females attend to Jenae. A crew of males yuck it up with Chase. And all is right as rain. Until a slow, steady clap.

CLAP...CLAP...CLAP...The room goes silent.

"Well, well, well," a voice blares from just inside the front door. "I thought this was a birthday party...instead it's an engagement."

Chase pushes one of his actor friends aside and brushes past two other colleagues just to confirm the voice...Eugene.

"Chase, my old friend. Happy Birthday," Eugene says. He gives Chase a bear hug.

"Come on, introduce me," Eugene says.

Chase is crippled. His tongue clogs. His throat chokes. He's scatterbrained. *How did he? Why is he? What if he tells them? Oh no, Jenae is staring at us.*

"He's overwhelmed folks. Ladies and gentlemen my name is Eugene Merriweather and this is my associate, Man-Man. But y'all don't mind him. He doesn't talk much."

The crowd gawks. Man-Man half-smiles. Chase notices Andrea's stock broker friend slip away onto the penthouse terrace.

"I'm an old friend of Chase's. From Georgia," Eugene says.

"Georgia?" Andrea blurts.

"Yes. Chase and I went to school together," Eugene replies.

"School together? Chase is from Boston," Andrea says.

Jenae rivets towards Chase. The conversation is in danger of rocketing in a direction he is ill prepared for. He thinks of something plausible.

"Uh, yes, yes Eugene and I became friends when my father got transferred to Savannah for a year," Chase says.

Eugene chimes in.

"Yes, but enough about us. Let me meet the gorgeous bride to be."

Eugene steps to Jenae. As she extends her arm for a handshake Eugene embraces her instead. He pulls them pelvis-to-pelvis. He takes a deep breath which forces his chest into her soft breasts. Jenae tenses up before gently breaking away. Chase is furious at the spectacle. He slaps his hand on Eugene's shoulder and squeezes. Eugene hides the pain of Chase's grip.

"Eugene's had a long trip so he's going to have to be going—,"

"But Chase, we should share some old stories. Like remember that time you owed this guy a debt because you got—"

"Hey, hey, hey you know what folks? It's been forever since I've seen this guy. Let me steal him for a bit. DJ Tanaka it's too quiet in here. This is supposed to be a celebration. Kick some tunes. I'll be right back folks," Chase says.

He ushers Eugene across the living room and into Andrea's kitchen. Man-Man shadows them inside. Andrea narrows her eye. She looks suspicious.

They walk down a short hallway of exposed brick before entering the kitchen. Andrea's marble countertops are cluttered with catered aluminum food trays. Man-Man is so tall he must duck under the copper bottomed Ruffoni cookware hanging above the center island. To their right is the floor-to-ceiling pantry. It has a thick, opaque burlap curtain instead of a door. Chase looks over his shoulder. Satisfied the music is loud enough to muffle his voice he snatches Eugene by the collar and pins him to the wall.

"Who the hell do you think you are coming in here like this?" Chase yells.

Man-Man slams his gargantuan paws on Chase's shoulders. As he is about to rip him from Eugene's neck…

"Wait, Man-Man," Eugene says. "Chase is just feeling a certain kind of way. And he's going to let go of me in the next five seconds. Unless he wants me to give his guests a more honest introduction. Who I *really* am and who he *really* is."

Chase's rage is tempered by his intellect. He relaxes.

"Good boy," Eugene says.

"I asked you a question Eugene," Chase yells.

Eugene wags his finger with a *tsk tsk tsk*.

"Take a chill pill playboy. Don't want your boujee, cheese sandwich eating friends hearing you get all niggerish do ya'?"

"You have no business coming here. How did you even know about birthday party?"

Eugene grabs a succulent hot wing from a tray. He sucks and chomps as he speaks.

"Twenty-first century, homeboy. People love telling their business on social media. They'll even give you directions to some *other* bitch's house. Ain't that some shit? Kids these days," Eugene says.

"Get out Eugene."

"Okay, let me explain something to you Mister Chase."

He tosses a chicken bone in the sink and snatches Chase by the jaw bone. His greasy, wet hot sauce fingers dig into Chase's cheeks..

"Stop fucking with me. Don't mistake my charming personality for friendship. Don't mistake patience for weakness. Don't. That's your word for the day, teacher boy. Don't. If you think about doing anything other than what I say remember your word of the day… don't."

"I'm doing *anything* for you."

"Okay. So you want me to tell that caramel cutie of yours the real deal? By the way them smitties of hers feel *damn* good."

Chase balls his fist and fixes to fire a blow.

"Eh,eh, eh. Don't get macho. Stay focused. Yeah I think I'll start with how you're not from Boston. Then this story about your parents. Then—"

Chase tries to calculate how he can escape from Eugene's sticky web.

"Relax, playboy. I see your mind racing. Looking for a way out ain't ya? Here's your exit strategy…Do what the *fuck* I say. See how simple that is? I even wrote it down for your candy ass."

Eugene nods to Man-Man who pulls out a scrap of paper. He presents it to Chase. Chase folds his arms and refuses to look.

"Oh stop being a bitch and read the goddamn note," Eugene says.

Man-Man shoves it in Chase's face. Chase removes the paper from between Man-Man's pudgy fingers. The note displays a woman's name, phone number and the address of the Marriott Hotel in Brooklyn. In the lower right hand corner is a room number. Chase shrugs his shoulders.

"And?" Chase says.

"And? And that's your first client, muthafucka."

"My first what?"

"Nigga, do we seriously have to go through this shit again?"

"Look—" Chase says.

"Look nuthin', goddamnit. I'm tired of this back and forth shit with you. Read it."

"I just did."

"Out loud, bitch. I wanna hear you say it. Just so we're clear as fuck. You seem to be confused about the difference between a request and a command."

"I just proposed to the woman I love. I'm not about to—"

"Gimme dat."

Eugene snatches the note.

"Jenae. Oh, Miss Jenae."

Eugene starts to walk out of the kitchen.

Chase cringes.

"Wait. Wait…just…wait. Let's uh—"

"Let's uh, nothing nigga. Here. Out loud. Now."

Fear, flight and fight all compete for dominance in Chase's mind. Fear wins. He reads the note:

"Vicky. +370-5-210-2222, Marriott Hotel, Adams Street, Brooklyn. Room 1203. Okay, why is this an international number?"

"Very good Chase. Quite observant. She's this foreign chick. In town for a week from one of them Russian European countries."

"How do you know her? What's her backgr—"

Eugene waves his hand as if Chase were a gnat.

"That don't matter. Remember your word for the day? She's paying cash money. That's all your punk ass need to know. Get it done next Friday. She said that's when she'll be most ripe."

"Ripe?"

"Goddamn dude really? You know…it's when a chick is ripe and ready…uh…what's the damn word Man-Man?"

Eugene snaps his fingers.

"Ovulating," Man-Man says.

"There you go. Ovulating, dummy. Unless you wanna have to keep dipping and spitting in the well? She's paying for the baby, not the baby making."

Chase puts his hand on the counter top and the other on his forehead.

"This isn't happening," he says.

"Oh, it's happening," Eugene says. He uses his fingers as tongs for another buffalo wing. "Just get it done. She'll hand you an envelope of cash. Now don't get stupid and forget to get the money just 'cause you want some free foreign tail."

"I don't want any of this, Eugene!"

Chase vise grips his scalp.

"Chase…Hey, playboy look alive. I need to hear confirmation that we have an understanding."

Chase sighs.

"How much am I supposed to get from her?"

"How much, isn't your concern. Just remember who you owe your life to and what happens if you don't play ball."

"Yeah, I know. But this one time. Just this one woman right?"

Eugene licks wing sauce from his fingers and wipes it on Chase's shirt.

"Tell the white girl that rents this place that those were some bomb ass wings. Let's go Man-Man."

As Eugene and Man-Man bop out of the kitchen Eugene turns back and says.

"One more thing. Happy Birthday."

He laughs and the two men exit.

Chase has no time to brood. He can't raise suspicions with a depressed face. He steps to the kitchen sink and turns the handle on the spigot. He cups the cool flow of New York tap into his palm. He cradles it into his mouth. Swishes and spits. He rinses the aftertaste of a bitter conversation from his jowls. He splashes and dries his feverish face, tucks in his shirt tail and strolls back into the fun.

"Hey buddy, we were starting to worry about you," Professor Scobee says.

"Worry? Me? Why? Why would you worry?" Chase says fidgeting. Jenae diddy-bops to the beat and cozies up to Chase.

"Relax babe, he was just wondering why you stayed in the kitchen after your friends left," Jenae says.

Chase grunts.

"Here hubby to be, I know you're not really a drinker, but it's our night so—"

Chase seizes the glass with both palms and gulps it all in.

"Whoa, whoa, slow down Mister. I like my men sober."

The party returns to its fever pitch as Tanaka switches to dancehall reggae. Two celebrations in one. Chase sips more wine. It

THE DONOR   88

takes the edge off. Jenae leads him onto the living room dance floor. It's time to get down. She lifts her elbows above her head and grabs the back of her neck. Her apple bottom teases a dirty dance. She backs her behind into Chase's stacked zipper. They slow grind to Dawn Penn's *No, No, No…You Don't Love Me*. Everyone eats, drinks and is merry. Almost everyone.

In the living room is a closed door. This door leads down a long semi-secret hallway that Andrea uses for storage. It runs adjacent to the kitchen. It's basically a square tube with an exit at the end. This open end leads into the back of the pantry. But instead of walling it up Andrea simply placed a five-shelf bookcase on wheels. You can roll it to the side and hear everything in the kitchen but remain unseen because of the burlap curtain mentioned earlier. And it is Andrea that emerges from the kitchen even though she never entered from it. She surprises Professor Scobee—who is busy devouring hot wings—when she pops out.

"Oh, I didn't even see you walk in the kitchen after Chase came out," he says.

She ignores him and goes to grab a glass of Sauvignon. She glues her pupils onto the booty bumping and crotch grinding between Chase and Jenae. And she zeroes in on Jenae's bedazzling ring finger. It flames her fury. But as Andrea's heart hollers, her mind plots. Because as she said earlier…she makes sure people get what's coming to them.

7 And The Pot Thickens

❧

KNOCK KNOCK

"Hello? You in here?"

The 1920's oakwood door, with the pockmarked glass pane, creaks open. Footsteps and chatter leech into his office from the hustle and bustle in the hallway. A pair of arched ginger eyebrows brows peek inside.

"Knock, knock?"

"Huh? Oh, Andrea," Chase says with a yawn.

"You need some coffee sleepy head?" Andrea says.

"No, no…I was just grading papers."

"Yeah right. You were daydreaming. And why is it so hot in here?"

"You know Tilden Hall got that project heat. Gotta crack the window even in winter. What brings you on this side of campus? Not used to you psychology department folks in the English department."

"I had a craving," she says.

She pauses her three and a half inch heels in front of the overstuffed bookcase.

"A craving?" Chase says.

"Mmmhmm."

Andrea chuckles as she thumbs through Michelle Alexander's *The New Jim Crow.*

"You find that book funny?" Chase asks.

Andrea cuts her neck.

"No, Chase. There's nothing funny about the mass incarceration of black men. I have this book on my nightstand. I was chuckling at *you*. You're afraid to ask what I was craving, aren't you?"

"Andrea, I don't have time for your—"

"Macaroons," she says.

"Macaroons?"

"Yes. From that shop you used to take me to around here. Le Petit something or another."

"Oh yeah. Le Petit León. Wow…that was—"

"Yes…*was*. Was, was, was." Her voice trails.

"So did you find it?" Chase asks.

"Find it? Oh, the pastry shop? Yes and no. It's been turned into one of those yogurt, crepe, wheatgrass places or something. I don't know."

"I bet you thought I was going to say *you* when I mentioned my craving huh?"

"Really? Andrea, listen."

"Relax, Chase. Proposing to your girlfriend in my living room last weekend made things *quite* clear as to where I stand."

Chase gasps.

"Oh my God, Andrea. It never occurred to me that you would… of course…of course you would have a problem with—"

"—have a problem with you getting on one knee and proposing to your current girlfriend in your *ex*-girlfriend's living room? Silly boy. Now what woman would have a problem with that?"

"Andrea—"

"At least you stepped your game up this time. Her ring had to be what? Four, five carats? *Twice* the size of the one you gave to me when you proposed?"

"Andrea, let me explain. I never thought you'd have an issue. I mean...come on. You and I were over a *looong* time ago. We decided we were better off as friends. Buddies. Come on we're homies now."

Chase gives her two fake punches on the shoulder as if she were his...*homie.*

No he didn't, Andrea thinks to herself. "So did you ever tell Jenae you were once engaged to your *homie?* Or was that too *looong* ago?"

"Andrea, I'm sorry. I just thought—"

"It's fine Chase," she says. She places her palm on his cheek. "I didn't come here for one of your puppy dog apologies. I actually came here to help."

"Help?"

"Tomorrow's your big day right?"

"Huh? What are you talking about Andrea?"

"Aww, don't be shy."

She slithers her nail across his shirt and inserts it through the second button. She feels his chest with her index finger. Chase pinches it away.

"I don't have time for your cat and mouse games. I know you didn't come all the way from our university's Lincoln Center campus in the city, just for some macaroons in Brooklyn. I'm sorry about proposing to Jenae in your apartment. I wasn't thinking. Okay?"

"You sound so sincere."

She rolls her eyes. Chase starts to plead his case again but Andrea closes her eyes and waves two fingers.

"I'm not here for that. Like I said, I'm here to help you. I heard your conversation."

"Conversation?"

"You and Eugene. I was in the pantry the whole time."

"Whoa. I should take a pic of your frozen face."

"You were...uh...what?"

"Listen, I have no idea what this guy has on you but—"

"I don't know what you think you heard Andrea, but—"

"Oh I know what heard. Hush up. Now, I don't know what Eugene has on you, or who this secret mystery man is that sent him —"

"Wait. How could you have been in the pantry without walking right past us? I could have sworn I saw you go into the bathroom from the corner of my eye."

"We'll get to *how* another time. I'm going to help you."

"I don't need, and I don't want, your help Andrea."

"Yes you do need it. We to manage the situation."

"Situation? You and I are not having this conversation. I need to go now anyway."

Chase walks to the door. Andrea snares his elbow.

"Did you even call that Vicky person?"

"Damn, you really *did* hear everything."

"We covered that already. Did you call her?"

"No."

"Well, call her and set up a time. 7 pm. My place."

"Your place?"

"Yes, my place."

"I'm *not* involving you."

"Right. Sure. Because you've been doing such a *bang up* job on your own?"

This last point causes Chase to reflect. *I have been trying to do this on my own and it's getting worse. One thing Andrea knows how to do is handle a situation to her advantage....hmmm...maybe if—*

"Okay, so hypothetically speaking, how exactly could you help?"

"I don't do hypotheticals. You set up the meet at my place."

"Your place? Why? She's staying at the Marri—"

"Shush. Three reasons. One, it allows us to control the environment. You don't know this woman do you?" Chase shakes his head. "Exactly. Two, my place protects you. I'll be there as a witness."

"A what? A witness? This isn't some sick threesome. I'm still trying to figure out how to keep this from being a *twosome.*"

"I won't be *in* the room with you. But trust me. I'll protect you."

"How are you going to—"

She shushes him again.

"And three? So I can create the right atmosphere for a woman."

"Atmosphere?"

"Yes, Chase. Atmosphere. What you think you're gonna do? Just hit it?"

"Honestly, I haven't even thought that far."

"See why you need me? You don't think. Why would a woman would a *service* like this, Chase? Why is she looking to get pregnant with a man she's never met before? Why not go to a doctor...a fertility clinic?"

"That's what I say. I thought the idea was crazy from jump but I don't have a choice. I can't explain why."

"And I don't expect you to. Somebody's got something major on you for the Chase I know to even *consider* this. But you can't look at this selfishly. It can't be a transaction. Women don't think like that. The right mood. Things go well. Stays private. And it's over with."

Andrea's confidence breathes an air of hope in his iron lungs.

"You always had this way of focusing on solutions to problems," he says.

Andrea skates a delicate finger down Chase's temple.

"Hmmm, someone hasn't used the razor this week."

"It's been that kind of week."

She cups his face and circles her thumbs over his stubble. The prickles remind her of their yesterdays. She leans closer and sneaks a sniff from his neck. Her nostrils remember the sweet spice of his manliness. She angles her mouth to his lips.

"Andrea don't."

He presses a gentle finger to her chin.

"Shhh," she says and plucks it off. She plants a borderline *just-a-friend* peck on the corner of his smile. Chase brushes himself back. Andrea smirks. She grabs her pink and plum Tory Burch handbag.

"I'll text you with instructions for Vicky. In the meantime? Please shave. You're scruffy. Oh, and one more thing."

"Yeah?" Chase asks.

"Relax. I have a plan for you."

She exits. Chase isn't sure what to make of her last point but for the first time all week he has something that has eluded him. Hope.

❧

SIZZLE...POP POP POP...SIZZLE

"Okay the pan is hot. Crack the eggs now," Chase says.

"I thought you said that was turkey bacon?" Devantay replies.

"It is."

"Sound just like swine to me. Smell like it to."

"*Soundz* and *Smellz* with an *s* young man. And we don't do pork on these forks," Chase winks.

"Am I stirring the eggs right?"

"Just about. It's all in the wrist," Chase says.

He places his hand on Devantay's wrist and guiding his egg beating technique. Chase mimics the bark of a TV chef.

"Skillet is hot. Sprinkle cheddar in eggs. Eye on those grits. Come on. Chop, chop!"

"Umm okay, okay," Devantay says.

"How dare you. What did you say?" Chase says.

"Oh, I mean…Yes Chef," Devantay replies with a salute.

The young boy pours the egg mixture into the pan. Chase begins to scramble them.

"I can do it myself," Devantay's pre-pubescent voice squeaks.

"But wait, we forgot the milk?" Devantay says.

"Milk?" Chase asks.

"Yeah…this guy at the group home says you should add milk to scrambled eggs. His name is Philip but he spells it funny. And it's really *Fuh-leep* with a long e. But we just call him, Cake."

"Cake?"

Chase places his hand on top of Devantay's hand with the spatula and adds more vigor to his egg stirring. Devantay snatches his wrist away.

"I can do it myself," he says.

Chase shakes his head with a smile.

"Why do you all call him Cake?"

"'Cause he's fat."

"Devantay!"

"Well he is."

Chase turns off the burners.

"Just because he's overweight?"

"It's because of 50 Cent."

"50 Cent?"

"Yeah. He's a rapper. You don't know who Fitty is? You old."

"I know who 50 Cent is Devantay."

"Well you know that line in his song, *21 Questions?*…I love you like a fat kid love cake? So we nicknamed him, Cake."

"That's horrible," Jenae says, standing in the kitchen doorway.

Chase and Devantay mirror startled looks at her.

"Babe," Chase sighs with droopy eyes.

"You were supposed to still be asleep," he says.

Jenae flashes her long eyelashes.

"Awww, my boo boo. Was him trying to suh-pwize him fiancée?"

She shuffles to Chase in her chenille slippers. Her burgundy robe hugs the boom and bounce of her curves.

"Come here my handsome, sensitive, thoughtful, surprise breakfast-maker-upper."

She tiptoes to him and plants a juicy one on his thick lips. Chase tugs her tight by her terrycloth knot. The fresh scent of her pomegranate and shea butter shampoo seeps into his hungry nostrils. Her hair has always been his catnip. And a creative expression of her soul. She switches hairstyles every other month and Chase always wants to sink his fingers inside. As they kiss, he inches into the nut brown forest of strands. Jenae quickly snaps her head back and smacks his hand. She waves a finger.

"Oh hell no. I love you, but you are not about to put those slimy, eggs 'n grits 'n butter fingers all up in the hair I just washed."

"Really?" Chase says, dumbfounded.

"What you mean, really? Yes, *really*," Jenae says.

"Black women and their hair," Devantay mumbles.

"Excuse me, Devantay?" Jenae says.

"Cake says you better not never touch a Black woman's hair. They turn into Jekyll. Or Hyde? One of them. Whichever is the crazy one."

Devantay concentrates on ladling just the right amount of food onto their plates.

"Hmph. You're lucky you're my favorite little guy," Jenae says. She kisses his forehead and grabs a thin wedge of turkey bacon.

The hickory and maple smoked aroma tunnels their nostrils. Jenae savors the smells. "Mmmm, reminds me of my Aunt Helen's country breakfast back in Ridgeland, South Carolina. We used to drive down there every summer with my grandmother as kids."

She strokes Devantay's day old barbershop haircut.

"This was supposed to be a surprise for you," Chase says.

Jenae puts on an exaggerated southern accent.

"Ooh, honey child it 'twas a surprise. Y'all got me feelin' like mint julep on the fourth of *Joo-Lie*."

She twirls and hugs herself like a scene from *The Sound of Music*. Chase cracks up.

"Keep going Miss Jenae, you're good," Devantay says.

"Sorry boys...that's all I got. I'm a lawyer not an actress. Now let's eat. I don't want my surprise breakfast to get cold."

They gather at the table and dig in. They converse about the latest law firm gossip and university happenings all while savoring mouthfuls of creamy grits and warm oven biscuits.

"This is like a family breakfast. At least I think it is. It's what I see in pictures," Devantay says.

The adults trade smiling eyes knowing how deep that statement was.

"You know Devantay? This *is* a family breakfast," Chase says.

"Oh, Chase don't forget... I have—"

CHIRP CHIRP CHIRP

"—I have that dinner with the partners of the law firm tonight. It must be a big deal. They called to confirm twice," Jenae says.

Chase is distracted by his smartphone's bird noise text notification. He grunts, *uh huh,* to Jenae. The text message says:

ANDREA

(1/2)

Spoke with Vicky. All set for 2nite.

Told her I was Eugene's asst.

```
     Be at my place by 6p.
             (2/2)
       She'll be here at 7.
     Wear the cologne I like.
    She'll like it 2. DONT B L8!
```

"Bad news?" Jenae says.

"Huh? No, no…just um…just a meeting I have to go to tonight," Chase says.

"A meeting? On a Saturday night? Dean Ganges must be lining you up for something big."

"Meeting? But Chase you're supposed to come to my talent show tonight remember?" Devantay says.

"Shit," Chase slams his fist on the table. He had completely forgotten about Devantay's show. Jenae and Devantay both look at Chase stunned. Chase never uses profanity around children.

"I'm sorry. I didn't mean to blurt like that. Look, I'm sorry little man. I forgot about this meeting. I have to go."

Devantay's eyes start to well up.

"Well…okay. But can you come instead then Miss Jenae?"

Jenae sighs and grabs the child's hand.

"I'm sorry sweetheart. I wish I could. That dinner with the partners is mandatory. I promise I'll—"

Devantay snatches his hand from her. He spits his food out and jumps from the table.

"Devantay?" Chase yells.

"What!" Devantay says.

"Excuse me?" Chase says.

Jenae tries to console the boy.

"Devantay, sweetheart listen."

"No. I knew this was going to happen. I told you what people do, Chase. You love people and they hurt you," Devantay says.

"Devantay, it's just that we're both busy tonight," Chase says.

"Yeah I know. Important meetings. So that means I'm not important. I'm not an important meeting," he says.

"Of course you are. It's just that something came up and we—"

"No, no, no, no," Devantay covers his ears and begins to hyperventilate. He kicks the chair and runs upstairs screaming. A door slams shut.

"Chase, why don't you just reschedule with Dean Ganges. She loves her star professor. She'll understand. How important of a school meeting can it be on a Saturday night?"

"Oh, so my meetings aren't as important as yours?" he snaps.

"Whoa...really? Where did that come from?"

"I'm sorry babe. That-that wasn't...that wasn't me," he says.

She takes a breath.

"You've been kind of jumpy ever since you proposed. If...if you're having second thoughts about marrying me—"

"No, no, no babe," he rushes to her. "It's not you. It's not the engagement. I'm just a little overwhelmed at work. Dean Ganges has been putting more on my plate lately."

"Tell you what. I'll call Octavia myself. We get along great. I'll cancel your meeting for you and you can put that little boy's heart back together again. Now where's my phone? Oh...you know what? I left it upstairs. I'll just use yours."

She grabs Chase's phone. It's something she does regularly without him ever objecting. Chase yanks her arm and pries the phone from her fingers.

"No, don't do that. I said this meeting is important."

Jenae sears an unblinking stare into Chase's eyes.

"Let. Go. Of. My. Arm. Now!" she commands.

Chase is puzzled until he eyeballs his own clutch. It shocks him. He hadn't realized he had grabbed her. He releases her arm. And for the first time ever…Chase has put his hands on Jenae.

"Babe, honey I-I-I didn't mean to—"

"Unh-Unh," she says through closed eyes and a shaking head. "You go to your meeting, Chase. You go handle your *important* business. Right now I'm going upstairs to calm a broken heart."

She tightens the belt on her robe and walks up the staircase. Chase sulks in the chair. His phone chirps again.

ANDREA

Hey. Did you get my txt? Confirm.

He looks at the screen. His eyes water. His bottom lip quivers. He thumbs a one letter reply.

CHASE

K

Chase rakes his fingers across his scalp and screams in silence. He devastated Devantay. He infuriated Jenae. All for a night with a Vicky. A woman he's never met. And he is about to wish he never did.

8 Vicky

❧

A chilly blast ruffles the dwindling leaves of bare branches. Chase tightens the noose on his camel wool waistcoat. His mind is cluttered with a past he cannot change, a present he cannot control, and a future in doubt. He shivers outside of Andrea's building. Fearful to move forward. Terrified to shift in reverse. He flips his collar and winces from the wind.

The door to the building bursts open behind him.

"What are you doing out here just lallygagging? You were supposed to be here an hour ago. It's almost seven. Get in here," Andrea says. Her crimson tresses snap like a flag in the windstorm.

Andrea shoulders the door against the 40mph arctic blast for Chase to come in. She whisks him through the antique lobby and into the vintage elevator. Andrea clangs the iron handle of the old school lift gate. The metal carriage jolts in its ascent. Andrea smacks Chase on his back shoulder.

"Hey, is this some kind of game to you?" she says.

"No," Chase says, stone-faced.

"Stop mumbling."

"I said no. And I'm not your child. So dial it back, lady."

They crawl past the second floor.

"What the hell were you doing? She could have shown up while you were standing outside looking stupid."

"Alright, I get it Andrea," Chase says.

"I don't think you do. Or maybe this isn't that big of a deal after all. Why don't you just tell me what Eugene's got on you?"

"Why? It won't change anything. Plus, it's none of your business."

"None of my business? Says the man riding up to *my* loft."

"Which was *your* idea. Ugh. Why is this damn elevator taking forever?" he says.

Chase fires his thumb into the third button over and over.

"That's not going to make it go any faster. You of all people should know."

"Don't remind me."

"Oh it's like that? That's your attitude? You better clean it up quick before she gets here or else you'll be doing this again."

"I don't know why I had to be here so early anyway. I just want to get this over with as quickly as possible."

"And that's precisely why your caveman ass needed to be here earlier. That kind of attitude is not very appealing to women."

The lift jerks to a halt. They step into the brick lined hallway with only one apartment door. Andrea punches in a six digit code on the security panel. Two beeps, a click and they enter.

"Gimme your coat," she says. She lays it on the cranberry leather sofa. "Here's the deal. We don't have much time so we'll have to do a crash course. Now when she rings the bell just buzz her in. Don't use the intercom. Don't let her hear your voice yet."

"Why? What's the big—"

"Shush," Andrea says, pursing her lips. "Creates an air of mystery. After you buzz her, stand over...there...no, wait not there... here, yeah here."

She positions him in the center of the room.

"Oh and take these." Andrea pops open a bottle of Pinot Noir and pours two glasses. "This is the top rated wine for a romantic evening. Cherry and black currant undertones with a hint of spice. Yummy and sexy," she says.

"You know I rarely drink."

"It's not about *you*. It's about the mood. Men don't understand that you start making love to a woman before you even touch her."

"This isn't a date, Andrea. This is business. Business I don't even want to do."

"Where's the romantic guy proposing to some other chick in his ex-girlfriend's living room?"

"Come on Andrea? I apologized for that and you said you were okay about—"

"I'm fine Chase. Let's finish this. Now when she comes in and sees you standing with these drinks, you say: *Hi Vicky, I'm Chase.* Nice and simple, see?"

"What do you mean when she comes in? Aren't you going to do the introductions?"

"Huh? Dude, are you for real? She won't even know I'm here."

"You said you would be a witness. In case there's a problem."

"I will be. I'll be in the pantry."

"The pantry? A witness in a pantry?"

"I'll be close enough to keep tabs, okay?"

Chase sighs. "Fine. This whole thing is so…ugh."

"Chase, just relax. That's your word for the day, okay? Relax."

"Why do I keep getting words for the day like I'm on Sesame Street?"

Andrea ignores his comment and walks about the room like a motivational speaker.

"Women are more in tune with emotion than men. We pick up on energy. So if you're relaxed, she'll be relaxed. But if you're tense she'll be tense. If it helps, just pour yourself a little more joy juice and go bottoms up. Now follow me."

Andrea leads Chase into the bedroom. Walls of exposed brick are dotted with a dozen black and white photographs in silver frames. All are nude silhouettes of lovers in various poses.

"Wow. This is different from the art you used to have on your bedroom wall," he says.

"Well, you haven't been in my bed in years now have you?"

Chase clears his throat. Andrea's micro-aggressions haven't escaped his attention. She has always been hot and cold towards him since their breakup. But her passive-aggressive comments increased when Jenae came into the picture. Chase reaches for the dimmer.

"Don't mess with the switch," Andrea snaps. "They're low for a reason. And I put two bowls of juicy, organic peaches, plums, and grapes on the dresser for you. Just in case you want to get...*creative*. I know how much you enjoy incorporating fruit," she says.

Chase sucks his teeth.

"Come on Chase. A lot of guys would see this as hitting the sex lottery you know."

"I'm not *a lot of guys* okay?"

Andrea reaches inside the bowl and pops a handful of plump red grapes in her mouth. As she chomps she gives a snarky reply.

"You're not as exceptional as you think you are."

BUZZ BUZZ BUZZ BUZZ

Chase jumps.

"Geez is that her?"

BUZZ BUZZ BUZZ BUZZ BUZZ BUZZ BUZZ BUZZ

"My God. The way she keeps ringing that buzzer sounds like you've got a real eager beaver on your hands, sweet cheeks."

Andrea smacks his tush. Chase flinches. She click-clacks her heels out of the bedroom.

He puts his head in a vise. *I can't believe this is happening. Jenae, the university, Devantay. Shit, and what if Eugene tells them all about the girl from Geor—?*

"Chase. Stop daydreaming. Come on."

Chase enters the living room.

"I just let her in the building. She's on her way up. You still don't want to tell me what this is all about?"

"I can't tell *anyone* what this is all about."

KNOCK KNOCK KNOCK

"Shit," they both blurt.

"Let me get a look at you. Oh come on Chase, fix yourself up. You're sloppy."

Chase fumbles with his shirt. As he zips, his shirt tail gets stuck in the zipper. He tugs at it furiously.

"Chase stop pulling. Just be still," she says.

KNOCK KNOCK KNOCK

"Yell to the door and say you'll be right there," she whispers.

"Huh?"

"Well, I can't say it. You're supposed to be alone."

"Right. Umm okay. 'C-Coming. One sec Miss," he says.

"Miss?" Andrea says. Chase shrugs.

Andrea drops to her knees and starts jerking on the zipper.

"This *so* not a good look," he says, angling down at her red crown.

"Focus," she says.

Andrea finally pops the shirt free. Chase zips up.

"Time to skedaddle. Remember, relax…and smile."

Andrea throws up a peace sign and slinks into the pantry.

Chase's hard bottomed Cole Haan casuals echo against the hardwood floors. He grabs the handle…exhales and opens.

And there she is. Vicky. Pale as plaster. She's raven haired, dressed in black and tall. Four inch stilettos put her eye-to-eye with Chase. More noteworthy than her height are her eyes. Striking. Or scary depending on your perspective. They are pitch black marbles floating in creamy pools of milk.

"Chess?" she says.

"Yes. I am Chase," he says, with the charm of an army private.

"I am Chase," Vicky says. She mocks him with robotic arm movements.

"Such a stiffy stiff. Are we just going to do this right here or are you going to invite me in?"

She has a European accent that Chase cannot quite place.

"Oh, of course. Please come in."

Her pace is deliberate. She scans the walls. Her facial expressions suggest she is impressed with the art. Although her face shows the wrinkles of a woman nearing forty, she hasn't a single strand of grey. Her straight and shiny black hair tapers to a V in the middle of her spine. She wears a form fitting velour mini-dress that hugs her svelte frame.

"What if there was something dangerous in here?" Vicky says.

Chase wrinkles his eyebrows.

"Dangerous? You're safe here. I can even leave the door open if that makes you more comfortable?"

"I said in here."

She pats the bulge of the alligator bag dangling against her hip.

"Uhhh…not quite sure where you're going with that question but we can—"

Vicky quickly sticks her hand inside, pulls out a silver pistol, and fires.

"BANG BANG BANG," she cries out.

Chase dives to his right. Andrea cracks the semi-secret hallway door open but suddenly Vicky grabs her stomach and cackles with laughter.

"Oh my hahaha. You should see your face. You are scared the shitless. It's just a gun lighter. Not real."

Chase is furious. Andrea snakes back into hiding.

"Are you fucking crazy? That's funny to you?" Chase screams.

She clacks her heels to him and shakes his shoulders.

"Come on. Loosen up."

She shakes him again and again. Chase grabs her wrists.

"Okay, enough. Joke over," he says.

"It is called the ice breaker," Vicky says.

Is this chick for real? Damn that Eugene.

"Are you ticklish, Chess?"

She pokes her bony index finger into Chase's armpit. He recoils.

"Oooh…you are. Tickle, tickle, tickle you. Tickle, tickle, tickle Chess." She curls all ten fingers as if to pounce. Her grin is psychotic.

It is at this point that Chase notices how Vicky's accent causes her to pronounce the name Chase like the word *chess*.

"You have a unique voice," he says.

Although it isn't one, she takes it as a compliment.

"Why, thank you. Most people think it is Russian," she says.

"Oh no, it's definitely not Russian," Chase says, not that he would know.

"You can tell? You impress me, *Chess*. But most people cannot figure out the accent. They start shouting the stupid countries like Austria. Do I sound like *The Terminator*? Or they insult me and say Poland. Poland? Only whores come from Poland."

Chase snickers. He knows Andrea can hear this conversation and her surname Lisi, is Polish.

"I am from Estonia. A sexy little country," she says.

She slides her hands down her unremarkable curves. Chase doesn't respond.

"You don't believe me sexy?"

"Oh no, of course…You're quite nice."

"Nice?"

"Sexy nice," he says with a forced smile.

"You know I need a drink. Yeah, let's have a drink. I hope you like Pinot Noir."

"Pinot Noir? You don't drink malt liquor?" she says.

Chase raises his left eyebrow but brushes the comment aside. He slurps a tiny sip from his glass. Vicky wastes gulps hers like a sports drink. She lifts the glass high and sticks out her canine tongue for the remaining drops. But she doesn't swallow. Without warning she grabs Chase's hand, sucks on his fingers, wipes her mouth with his palm and growls. Chase's expression is one of shocked horror. He tries to shift the energy of the room.

"Soooo are you hungry?" Chase says.

Vicky peeks down the hall towards Andrea's bedroom.

"We don't need small talk, Chess. Is that the bedroom?"

Chase tries to stall.

"What kind of guy would I be if I didn't feed you? I think she…I mean I think I have some—"

"Is it down this hall?" She starts walking. "Come along, *Chess*."

Vicky disappears into the bedroom. Chase paces in front of the sofa.

Psst…Psst…Psst.

Andrea pops her head in from the kitchen.

"What the hell are you waiting for? Get in the bedroom."

"Andrea, this chick is looney tunes. I'm not going in there with her."

"Yes you are. Get in there and get it over with. Get the money and you'll be one step closer to getting Eugene off your back."

"This isn't easy Andrea."

"Stop bitching. Women have been having sex with Men they didn't like for thousands of years. So…*woman up.*"

Chase attempts to protest but Andrea silences him.

"Chess…oh Chess," Vicky says from the bedroom. "Come boy. Come."

"Boy? *Boy*? Did you hear that? This is the second suspect comment she's made." he says.

"Stop making something of nothing. She's European. They talk weird."

"I bet you didn't say that when she called your Polish people a bunch of whores."

"Dude, just go handle your business," Andrea says.

She fans her palms towards the bedroom and disappears in the kitchen. Chase tries to psyche himself up for the task at hand:

Okay it's just a thing.

Like a job.

It's not something you WANT to do.

You're being forced so you're not really cheating on Jenae right?

Yeah…that's it. I have no choice.

He marches down the hall and into the bedroom door. The air is floral and spicy. Bergamot and sandalwood candles burn on the dresser. Chase glances at the bed. It is empty with the exception of a large white envelope on the pillow. He looks around the room but Vicky isn't present. Andrea's room is large, vast in fact—but it isn't a maze. He knocks on the door of the master bath. No answer. He enters but it's empty. He even checks behind the shower curtain.

This chick can't be hiding?

"Come on Vicky this is ridiculous."

He sits on the mattress. He opens the envelope and peers inside. It is stuffed with stacks of $100 bills. *Damn. There's got to be at least 20 G's in here.*

"Come on, Vicky I know you're in the walk-in closet okay? So just come out."

Really? She's actually going to make me get up and walk over to the clos—CLICK. Just as Chase rises he feels a cold steel clamp on his right ankle. He looks down just in time to see a thin pale arm retreat underneath the bed.

"What the hell? Handcuffs?"

She tee hees like a banshee.

Chase tries to walk but the other cuff is attached to the iron bedrail. He tries to lift Andrea's super heavy bed but his angle is too awkward. He can't square himself.

"Okay, Vicky stop this. Come out from under the damn bed."

Vicky stretches her wiry arms from under the box spring. And then her spindle legs. She creeps from underneath like a tarantula. Instead of standing upright she rises by gradually unfolding her body limb by limb. She has disrobed down to a leather bra, thong and her silver stilettos. As she burns a weird stare into Chase's eyes she mimics the sound of a guitar.

"Bing Bonga Bing Bong Bong…Bong Bong Binga Bong Bong Bong." She dances and snakes her limbs in the air as if she were trying to hypnotize him with rubber.

"Wait…are you? Are you humming the *James Bond* theme? Okay, that's it. Listen, I think we should—"

SMACK

Vicky whacks an open palm, plum across Chase's cheek.

"Silence. You have not been given permission to speak," she says with melodrama.

The smack sends Chase falling backward onto the mattress. With his ankle still shackled, Vicky pounces and splits her thighs on top of him. She grabs his throat and starts to grind on the limp lump of his zipper.

"Okay, enough. That's it. Vicky I said stop."

She refuses to comply so Chase grabs her arms and tosses her off. She laughs.

"Sooo, *Chess* likes it rough. Rough he likes it...rough, *ruff, ruff, ruff.*" She barks like a dog.

"What the hell?" Chase says.

"Chess, Massa is angry now. You will have to *beg* for my love... Beg. Beg me now slave boy."

"What? *Massa! Slave boy!* Okay, first the malt liquor comment, then boy, now this slave massa shit?"

"Shut up. I'm the Master. You are the slave. You are acting like this is racial. It's fantasy. Now play your part. I paid for you."

"Are you *that* clueless? Do you *not* get the optics of this?"

"We had a deal." She pokes him repeatedly in the forehead.

Chase swats her wrist and sits on his elbows.

"Forget your deal. Go to a clinic."

"No. He said I get a pretty, mixed baby. European hair, exotic *light* brown skin. And I get the sex any, which way I want. You don't get that at a clinic. You have your money. You are messing up this. Messing. Messing. Messing. Argh."

She screws her forefingers into her temples as if she has a migraine. Her pale skin turns pink.

"Hey, hey it's alright. I understand. I'm sorry for not behaving."

He holds her wrists and kisses the back of her palms. He leans in and nibbles on her earlobe. It excites her. She tugs on his buckle.

"Umm...Master wait? I have something very, very special for you. But you have to uncuff me to get it. If you do then I can give it to you...give it to you good. Two words...Black. Buck."

Vicky's eyeballs rocket from their sockets. She slips her hand underneath the pillow and retrieves a tiny key. She stares at Chase. Chase stares back and roars. Vicky hops off, drops to the floor, and unlocks the metal cuff on his ankle. She jumps back to her feet ready and eager.

"Give massa her stallion."

Chase jumps up. Vicky shuts her eyes, closes her ankles, and stretches her arms like a crucifix. She exposes her throat waiting for Chase to ravage her. He shoves her aside. He grabs the money, her pile of clothes and gathers them in a bunch.

"What the hell are you doing?" Vicky says.

"Here. Take your shit. Take your crazy. And get the fuck out."

"You lied. You lied to me," she yells.

"Welcome to America. It's what we do."

Vicky refuses to budge. A thin green vein of anger bulges down the middle of her forehead.

"Look lady, you can stand there mean-mugging me all you want to but your ass is still—,"

HACH...TUCH...SPIT

Vicky vomits a glop of spit in his eye. It slimes down his cheek like watery snot.

"Alrighty then...okay...yup...real nice. Real psycho-chick nice," He bites his bottom lip with a smile that isn't a smile.

He wipes the saliva from his face with Vicky's velour dress.

"You idiot. That's a Valentino," she screams with a kick to his shin.

"Argh...you crazy b—"

Chase grabs his leg and hops around on one foot.

"You know what? You know what, lady?"

Chase flips Vicky over his shoulder and fireman carries her out of the room, down the hall and into the living room. Shouts of, *we had a deal,* and threats of Russian mafia retribution echo. He carries her out the front and drops her and her stuff in the empty elevator like a sack of potatoes. He presses the lobby button. Just before the gate closes, a stiletto whizzes by his temple. The lift rumbles down to the sounds of foreign language curses. Chase trudges back into the apartment. Andrea is standing inside the doorway, arms folded, shaking her head.

"Wow. I wish I had some popcorn to go with that show," she says.

"You slither from your little bat cave with jokes instead of help?"

"She would have gone nuts if some strange woman she didn't know was here jumped in."

"She *already* went nuts."

Chase heads into the kitchen and splashes cool water on his brow. He catches his reflection in the window pane above. Three popped buttons and a ripped collar. He throws up his hands.

"Great. Just great," he says.

Andrea hands him a sweater.

"Here. It's from…well…our past. I saw her rip your collar. You should probably wear something you wouldn't need to explain."

"Thanks. Wait, how could you have seen that she ripped my shirt all the way from the pantry?"

Andrea doesn't respond.

"Whatever. Honestly, I could really use a drink now," he says.

"Oh, the Pinot is on the counter," she says.

"Not that kind of drink. I need something soothing," Chase says.

"Oh. I should have some chamomile tea in the pantry," Andrea replies.

As Chase goes to the pantry Andrea has a sudden realization. She attempts to tug him back. But she's too late.

"No, wait Chase, I'll get it for you," she says in a panic.

Chase opens the burlap curtain and flicks the light revealing a stool and a smart tablet propped on a shelf. The screen is illuminated with a streaming video of Andrea's bedroom. Chase squints to the screen like Mister Magoo. He glares at Andrea.

"Is this—? You put a camera in the bedroom? Watching me?"

"Chase, listen it's not a—"

"It's not a camera? Is that what you're about to say?"

"It's not a *camera* camera."

"What the hell does that mean?"

"It's a camera, but it's not for me. It's for you."

"For me? Just because I'm being blackmailed doesn't mean I'm stupid."

"Chase you're not listening."

"Get out of my way. I have a two nut job per night limit. Bye."

Andrea runs after him.

"Chase, the camera *is* for you. Did you ever stop think what would happen if one of these women said you did something to them? Against their will? Or if they turned out to be crazy like this chick? Wouldn't you want proof that you didn't do anything wrong? That's what I meant when I said that I would be a witness."

He pauses.

"I never considered that. Why didn't you say that from jump?"

"Dude, you stood outside for an hour. You were nervous enough as it is."

Andrea palms his cheek and smoothes his chest. Although her moment of tenderness is familiar, she's not Jenae.

"I...I've got to go. I just gotta figure some things out."

He grabs his coat, walks out and presses the elevator button. The lift arrives and he heads down to the lobby.

Andrea walks back into the kitchen and pours herself a drink. She grabs the smart tablet, opens her web browser and logs into an account.

"Ah...video saved...press upload...and done Mr. Archibald."

9 Guess Who's Coming To Dinner?

TINK TINK TINK TINK TINK.

The metal spoon rattles the wine glass as it's raised to the chandelier. The Blue Mosque in Istanbul inspires the tiled walls of the private dining room. The linen table cloth has just been cleared of sixteen empty plates. Only the flecks of tasty, Turkish kebabs, a few grains of tomato and cilantro bulgur rice, and a pile of clay oven pita bread remain. Bloated tummies accompany bloated conversations. *The Anatolia.* It is Brooklyn's only Tristar Chevron rated banquet hall. Chase and his colleagues eagerly await the final course—honey drizzled baklava.

"Okay, okay enough of your ivory tower banter you paper revolutionaries," Dean Ganges bellows.

She addresses the room with the sharp, booming diction of a one woman Broadway show.

"I have been honored over the past thirty years to be the chairperson of Brooklyn University's Department of English—and for the past ten years as the liaison betwixt our respective disciplines."

Professor Scobee leans into Chase's ear with a mouthful of kebab, "I love how she talks. Who still says betwixt?"

"But true leadership is knowing when to usher in fresher, bolder voices. Thus, it is with a bitter sweetness that I announce my retirement from the university."

A smattering of *Oohs* and *Whats* reverberate around the table. Chase himself is surprised.

"I will finish the academic year but I am prepared to name my successor. Recently ranked number one in *Brooklyn Professional Magazine's*, Thirty under 30…please welcome Brooklyn University's incoming Department Chair of English…Professor Chase M. Archibald."

Chase receives a standing ovation. He gawks at Dean Ganges like an overwhelmed game show contestant. She has never even hinted at retiring and Chase certainly never considered himself for the position.

"Stand up professor. This is where you make your acceptance speech," she says.

Chase is awe struck. As he rises to address the table, the door flies open. A blaring voice rushes in like a rogue wave.

"Well, congratulations Professor Ar-Chee-Bawld," a wide-eyed Eugene announces. He saunters in with the same slow hand clap as when he crashed Chase's birthday party. Man-Man soon follows.

Chase does his best to contain dual feelings of fear and rage as his right palm chokes the edge of the table linen.

"What are you doing here Eugene?" Chase says, through a clenched grin.

"Aren't you going to introduce me?"

"Eugene, we're in the middle of a meeting."

"I know. You see I've been trying to get in touch with you for the past three weeks. Phone, email, knocks on your door. But no Chase."

"Everyone this is my old friend Eugene Merriweather. Some of you met him at my birthday party. Eugene my apologies for not returning your—"

Eugene raises his hand.

"No, it's okay. You're a busy man. So, I tracked you down at the school. The department's secretary…Carol I believe? She said you were having this big year-end faculty dinner. I explained who I was, she gave me the details, and here I be. I wish I would have known about your promotion. I could have told our father about it when I flew down to see him last week," Eugene says.

Chase grimaces. Dean Ganges is puzzled.

"Father? Chase...Eugene is your brother? Wait, your parents died though," she says.

Chase's mocha skin turns reddish brown. Eugene smirks. He makes Chase stew in his anxiety before breaking the pause.

"No, Dean Ganges. We're not brothers by blood. After Chase's father—ahem—died, *my* father treated him like the son he never had. Funny, considering I'm the son he actually *did* have? But hey...you can't pick your parents. Dean Ganges, everyone...my apologies for the interruption, I'll leave."

Chase starts to escort Eugene out.

"Oh but Dad has a message for you Chase. Should I tell you outside?...Wait, you know what? You folks are having such a nice dinner. I'll just spit it out for everybody to hear. How about that Chase?"

"Uh no, no that won't be appropriate. Dean Ganges this will only take a few minutes. Is that okay?" Chase says.

He pauses for her response. She nods, but her lack of a *verbal* yes is not a good sign. Nonetheless, the three men walk out and into the carpeted hall. Eugene starts to speak.

"Not here," Chase says. "Follow me."

They power-walk down the corridor and around a bend. Chase stiff arms a pair of swinging double doors labeled employees only. It leads into a drafty tunnel. The cinder block walls are cold and damp. The muffled clang of dishes and mumbled foreign conversations echo from the far end. Dimly lit, amber bulbs dangle from the pipes above. They cast a harsh shadow on Chase's biting expression.

"What the hell do you think you're doing Eugene?" Chase says. He steps nose-to-nose. Man-Man jumps to intervene but Eugene calls him off.

"Negro, please. I can smell the Similac on your breath."

"I asked you a question," Chase says.

"Why I crashed your snooty college dinner? I guess because someone wasn't taking me seriously. So I went to visit my father."

"You went to see Bam?"

"Yup. And I updated him on your bullshit."

Chase squints an eye and crosses his arms with suspicion.

"You know I've been thinking, Eugene."

"Don't think. Leave that to me."

"Bam looked out for me when were in Georgia. And he got me set me up in Brooklyn. So, why would he send you all the way up here just to mess that up?"

"Let's just cut to the chase. Excuse the pun."

"Wow, he knows what a pun is," Chase says.

Man-Man smacks Chase upside the head. He lunges back at the four hundred pound henchman. They tussle in the claustrophobic space. Eugene jostles in between them.

"Chill, chill. Break it up. Break it up I said…Man-Man let go of Chase's face."

The giant removes his catcher's mitt palm from Chase's entire head. Chase breathes heavily.

"Are you done with your hero moment? Now, let's get back to business. Yeah, Bam took care of you."

"Which is why this whole scheme doesn't make sense."

"So you don't believe you owe anything? People do favors out of the goodness of their hearts? Your whole world is an act, Chase. We can shut your concert down in a finger snap, playboy."

"Your threats don't scare me. I'm starting to think Bam didn't even send you. Why would he jeopardize what he helped create?"

"We about making that money. All you had to do was your part. You forget what your world looked like after that snowflake down south?"

"I'm done. I know Bam. And I know you. This whole thing sounds more like *you* than *him*. You go ahead and try to blow up my spot but by going back in my dinner meeting. Test me if you want to."

Chase turns to rejoin his colleagues.

"Not so fast, playboy. I thought your punk ass might be trying to put on the big boy pants since I ain't heard from you."

Eugene snaps his fingers at Man-Man. The behemoth slides his bear claw inside his triple XL leather coat. Chase can hear the gargantuan's stubby fingers fumble for something metallic. Chase squares up expecting the worst. Man-Man hunches. Chase hunkers. Man-Man looks from side-to-side, and whips out a black metal wafer. He displays it like a tray of food. It's just a digital recorder.

"Well you certainly have a flair for the dramatic," Eugene says to Man-Man. Man-Man snorts.

"I told my father about our lack of progress...*your* lack of progress to be exact. Well, you know Angelo "Bam" Hickson. Wasn't too pleased about that. What was that word he kept saying Man-Man?...Oh I remember now...*ungrateful*. Just in case you had doubts I recorded him. Listen for yourself."

Eugene holds the recorder high and hits play. Chase instantly recognizes the clear and angry baritone of Bam Hickson in the middle of a tirade against him:

```
I don't ask, I tell. Somebody didn't get
the memo? Somebody needs some reminding
as to who the fuck I am? What I can do?
Defying me? Me? I don't take that. Not
from someone that owes me their life
[AUDIO DISTORTION][Bam's fist slamming a
table] —would have been ripped to shreds
if it weren't for me. I created
[DISTORTION] —Chase. I built Ch-
```

```
[DISTORTION]Chase.  And   I   can   break
[inaudible]  him.   No  one  defies  me.  His
[DISTORTION]  career?  Over.  A  little  boy
he  mentors?  That's  done  too.  Getting
married  to  [DISTORTION]  a  lawyer?  I  will
destroy  her  too.  [DISTORTION]  —Chase
better  do  this  or  I  will  expose
[inaudible]  who  he  really  is.
```

Bam's voice detonates into a frenzy of expletives and restatements about he can do. The sound of furniture being shoved is followed by a hacking and gurgling sound. Eugene presses stop. Chase leans against the cinder wall and bows. He misjudged, underestimated and miscalculated.

"That last sound you heard? That was him choking me," Eugene says.

Chase looks up.

"Yeah. That's how angry he was at *you*. You weren't in front of him so he took it out on me. As usual."

"I-I had no idea he would—he's never b—"

"—Been like that with you?" Eugene interrupts.

"Yeah."

"That's because you were the golden child. You never experienced the real Bam Hickson. But we don't have time for this Dr. Phil shit. That chick you sent away was worth twenty grand."

"She was a racist nutcase," Chase says.

"Stop whining. She wasn't racist."

"Wasn't racist? She wanted me to be her slave and call her massa."

"Look, choir boy that's not *racist*...that's just role play. *Normal* people do kinky shit like that."

"Eugene, she smacked me in the face and spit a loogie in my eye."

"Damn."

"Yeah, damn."

"Uh…okay, I'll give you that one. But look it's all good. We've already worked the kinks out going forward."

"So what does Bam want me to do next?" Chase asks.

"Bam? Nah. *We,* means me and that redhead snowflake of yours."

"Redhead snow—? Wait…hell no. Andrea? How the hell are you talking to Andrea?" Chase says.

"She called me."

Eugene pops a piece of chewing gum in his mouth.

"Called you? How did she even get your—"

Eugene snaps his fingers to Chase's face.

"Hey! Cupcake. Stay focused. *How,* ain't important. Sort that out later. But she's gonna help. Make everything easy."

"This is not happening," Chase says.

"Get a grip. Red is gonna get the chicks now. Find them, screen them, make sure they're not a bunch of Dodo birds."

"She'll what? Hell no. Whatever. I'll deal with Andrea myself."

"Do I need to replay this tape? You *do* realize who you're fucking with don't you? Fine. Whatever, macho man. I'll play this tape for that Dean Ganges of yours right now. Since you all bold and shit. You bold and shit now, right?"

Chase doesn't respond.

"Good. Now, your redhead is going to get these chicks for you. You just be a man and do what men do. Can you manage that?"

"How?" Chase says.

"What do you mean *how*? Don't know how to screw?"

"You're a crass little man. How is she going to get these women? I don't want a repeat of the first one. Which reminds me. How the hell did you find that Vicky woman, anyway?"

"Oh that's easy. The internet. Ever heard of it?"

"This is funny to you?"

"Listen, I'm a humble brother. I can admit a tiny mistake. My bad, okay? We just need to make a...uh...course correction."

"A course correction? Involving Andrea is a course correction?"

"She found *me* bruh? At first I thought it was weird but then she started to make a lot of sense. She knows you well. And she knows how to plan shit. I'll say that much."

"Oh, she will be my *first* call, believe me."

"Whatever. Just don't fuck this up. Anyway, Me and Man-Man gotta bounce. Red got your instructions for next weekend."

"Next weekend?"

Eugene and Man-Man exit the way they came in.

Chase's pocket vibrates. He fumbles for his phone and sees:

```
                  Dean Ganges
You need to get back. Not a good 1st impression 4
                 the next Chair.


                    Chase
        Sorry, Dean. Coming now.
```

He straightens his tie, tucks in his shirt and puts on a fake smile for his troubled soul.

10 Double Trouble

✧

A butterscotch bosom slumbers on a warm mocha chest. Their bodies appear gift wrapped in a silk ribbon. The lovers lay in a dreamscape. That peaceful place of—

BUZZ BUZZ BUZZ

Technology. It's like grandpa prodding his cane in your side, demanding the remote. The vibrating phone pokes a finger his in brain and disturbs him from his sleep. His groggy fingers fiddle on the nightstand. Loose change. A sock. Aloeswood incense.

"Chase get the phone," Jenae groans from under the frumpy pillow.

The buzzing stops just as he lays eyes on the screen.

ANDREA

(3) Missed Calls

He wipes the crust from his eyes and peaks over his back shoulder to make sure his frizzy haired beauty is still buried under her pillow. He cradles the phone from any surprise gaze and thumbs a text:

CHASE
Andrea. Why you keep calling?
Cant talk. CB L8tr.

Chase puts the phone—screen side down—on the nightstand. He's now wide awake. He eyes Jenae. He loves to admire her. Especially after dawn when her beauty is at its most natural.

Chase slides a finger from the nape of her neck to the rising dune below her back. He slips the sheet off and climbs on top. His knees sneak between her thighs and splice them apart. As she lays on her stomach he removes her pillow and nosedives into her curly follicles. *Mmmm,* the nutty butters with hints of anise, rivet his nostrils. Her sleepy breaths go silent. He knows she is awake. He sits up on his knees and pulls her bottom up to his face. She provides little assistance. He licks and laps. But she utters no sound. Nor does she shiver or tremble or moan. Even her breaths are mute. Chase takes no notice of these non-reactions. He assumes she is feeling the pleasure of his tongue. That would be a false assumption.

"Stop," she says.

He slurps.

"Chase I said stop."

Chase ignores her commands and grips her hips. Jenae reaches her arm behind her and smacks him. She wriggles away. Chase is dazed. Dazed more from her emotion than from the blow.

"Babe, wh-what's wrong? Did I hurt you?"

Jenae pulls her knees to her bare chest and wraps them.

"Babe. Babe, what did I do?"

Jenae refuses to eyeball him. He reaches to caress her but stops himself. Instead he locks their knuckles and pauses with patience. He doesn't say a word. He just waits for her. After a moment. She speaks.

"Who was on the phone, Chase?"

"What do you mean? What's going on?"

Chase is perplexed. Jenae never questions him. She takes her hand back and turns over. In their three years together, this is a new experience for him.

"Chase? Something's different."

"What do you mean, different?"

She doesn't respond.

Chase walks over to her side of the bed and crouches. He strokes the curls from her eyes. They are glassy. He kisses her tears. Lets his lips linger to sip the salty trickles. He plants a tender peck on her forehead and proceeds to nibble her nose.

"Stop, that tickles," she coos.

Chase smiles.

"Don't look at me like that, " she says.

Chase knows she's warming up but wonders if she suspects.

"Talk to me baby?" he says.

"Alright. Well…last weekend you called me about the faculty dinner when I was at my law conference in D.C. right?"

"Yes, my promotion. You weren't happy about that?"

"No, of course I'm happy for you. It's just. It's just I had some great news of my own too."

Chase lights up.

"Well? Come on, share, share."

Jenae half-smiles.

"We had a company dinner Saturday night. The partners told me how well regarded I was. How they really took notice when I refused to take plea deals in the Prospect Park Three case. I stuck to my guns and got acquittals for those boys whose *confessions* were coerced by the cops. They were impressed. So last weekend they made me an offer to become partner."

"Babe, that's—that's amazing."

Jenae's face is shows no joy. Chase notices.

"There's a but, isn't there?" he says.

Jenae nods.

"Oh, the distance? I'm a professor in Brooklyn you would need to be D.C.? Babe we can work all that out."

"No, not that."

"So, what is it?"

"Why didn't I want to rush to tell you? The man I love. I'm hesitating even now."

"Wow…yeah. I guess that is a good question. So, why?"

"I don't know. Something just seems off between us. Frankly, ever since the night you proposed. When your friend showed up."

Jenae's last line rattles him. He starts to panic inside and wonders if she saw something, heard something or if that annoyingly accurate radar known as female intuition is at play.

Chase's phone vibrates again. By reflex he glances at it before returning his gaze to Jenae. Too late. Her glare is menacing.

"Why are you looking at me like that?" Chase says.

The phone continues to buzz. He silences it.

"That's the fourth time your phone has gone off. That's unusual for you."

"What do you mean? This is only the second time this morning."

"Yeah. *This morning*. It rang twice overnight."

Chase has a blank stare.

"Babe, you've never acted like this bef—"

RING RING RING

RING RING RING

"The landline now? Really? Crack of dawn?" she says.

"I'll take care of it," Chase says.

He reaches for the receiver. Jenae intercepts.

"Hello," she says.

Chase pantomimes a…*who is it?* Jenae holds her hand to his face.

"Excuse me?…How am I? Oh I'm just full of joy and happiness. And yourself?…Oh that's *sooo* good to hear…Yeah he's right here… oh, of course you can speak to him. He's been expecting your *fifth* call."

Jenae stiff arms the phone to Chase.

"Take the damn phone Chase," she says. "I'm going in the shower."

Jenae stomps into the bathroom. Chase hears the *squeak—squeak* of the faucets followed by a steady spray.

"What," he barks into the receiver.

"Don't *what* me? I've been calling and texting for hours."

"Yeah, my *fiancée* made that abundantly clear."

"Don't get mad at me because you can't handle your chick."

"Why are you blowing up my phone anyway?"

"We got stuff to go over. Your date tonight at my place?"

He lowers to a gravely whisper…"Don't call it a date."

"It is what it is. Don't muck it up like you did last time."

"Like *I* did? Look, I have *zero* interest in doing this."

"I'll give you a trick from when I took theater as an undergrad. What you've got to do is get out of your head. Forget school, Devantay, and especially forget about Jenae. You've got to become someone else. A character. Don't think of yourself as Chase. Think of yourself as…I don't know…Bob."

"Bob? Who the hell is Bob?"

"Dude, work with me here. Call him whatever you want. But for this to work you must use a truth. Find something honestly appealing to you about this woman. Then use that one truth to become Bob. That was your problem with the last one. You didn't try to find something you actually *liked* about her."

"Because there was just *so* much to like about the Russian racist."

"She was Estonian."

"Whatever, Andrea."

"Chase, focus."

"That artsy mumbo jumbo makes no sense. You're basically telling me to find the truth in a lie?"

"You just passed Acting 101."

"Whatever. This is a damn nightmare."

"Just be on time, Chase. Goodbye."

He slams the phone in the charging cradle and walks to the bathroom. Chase knows he needs to smooth things over with Jenae. He comes up with a thought: *I'll make her that breakfast we had at the cabin in Vermont. Sweet apple crepes with homemade vanilla whipped cream, eggs Benedict and her favorite hot matcha green tea.*

He tightens the robe around his waist and runs downstairs with a proud smile. Hearing that Chase has left the room the bathroom door creaks all the way open. What Chase noticed was that the door was never fully closed to begin with. Jenae steps out. Her skin and curls should be glistening from the shower. But she's as dry as a bone. Not a bead. Not a drop. Just a dried tear under a sad eye.

The white moon illuminates the dark sky. An old hip-hop song says that this is when the freaks come out. But Andrea's Brooklyn street is deserted except for an idling black Town Car waiting for a fare and the bearded Chasidics shuffling home on the sabbath.

His wood bottomed soles scrape the cement as he treks from the subway to the loft. It is the most calm he has felt all day. Jenae was quiet at breakfast. Standoffish in fact. She gave only one word responses to his attempts to converse. The fancy breakfast was a yawn. Chase did find it odd however, that after twenty minutes of monosyllabic answers to questions, Jenae would fire a question:

> *"Hey, why don't we catch a movie tonight?"* Jenae said.
> *"Oh, sorry babe. I have to help Tanaka. He has a gig in the Hamptons tonight and his assistant bailed on him."*
> As Chase continued to embellish the lie, Jenae reached over the breakfast table and pressed two fingers to his lips.
> *"Never mind it's okay,"* she said. And walked upstairs.
> But when a woman says to a man, *it's okay,* and walks away? It's *not* okay.

Chase reaches Andrea's building. She buzzes him up. Her door is ajar. He enters but winces from a sudden blast of loud music. Bopping and twirling in the middle of the floor is Andrea. She dangles a half empty glass of chardonnay. She dances over to Chase and twerks her behind below his belt buckle.

"Okay, okay settle down. Someone's already turnt up I see." He puts distance between their pelvises.

"Settle down. Shit, we're just getting to know each other."

"We?" Chase says.

Andrea points toward a young woman leaning on the bookcase. She's thumbing the pages of James Baldwin's *The Fire Next Time*. She's short but not tiny. Her elastic jeans shrink-wrap her thick thighs and muscular calves. She sports vintage Air Jordans, and a cleavage blaring red tee. Her colossal bouquet of hair is a gorgeous throwback to a 1970's Pam Grier. Her crown is pushed back from her face with a headband in a Trinidadian flag design. Andrea turns the music down.

"Hi, Chase. I'm Evelyn," she waves.

Her chestnut cheeks beam an explosion of cheer. She has the kind of smile that should be followed by a starburst and a *PING*.

She marches over to Chase with a firm handshake.

"Wow, strong grip," Chase says.

"You can thank Dad for that. Ahem… *People form an impression of you in the first 15 seconds of meeting you. Make sure your handshake says you are a woman who handles business,*" Evelyn says, mimicking a Trini man's cadence.

Chase chuckles.

"You do that well," Chase says.

Andrea circles the wine in her glass and studies them.

Evelyn is a fireball. She has a big personality for a petite woman. She has an alluring physique but it is her outgoing nature that attracts Chase. He feels like a married man eyeing the hot chick at the end of the bar. He twirls his empty ring finger.

"Drink?" Andrea has Chase a ginger beer.

"No wine for you Chase?" Evelyn says.

"Chase don't drink. He'll massage that non-alcoholic soda all night," Andrea says.

"Well, I hope that won't be the only thing he massages," Evelyn says.

Andrea raises an eyebrow and winks. She stumbles to Chase's ear and whispers.

"Mmm. You see that bootaaay? And who wouldn't wanna juice that rack? Bob better work those lovely jubblies tonight," she slobbers.

"Stop being ignorant, Andrea. You're piss drunk."

Evelyn grabs her wine and sits on the couch. Chase remains standing next to Andrea. She elbows him.

"Ouch!"

"Go sit next to her, stupid."

"Evelyn, I'll be right back sweetie. I've got goodies in the kitchen," Andrea says and leaves them be.

Chase takes a swig of his ginger brew and sits by Evelyn.

At least she didn't jump out from underneath the furniture like the last cray cray," he says to himself.

"Penny for your thoughts?" Evelyn says.

"Me? Oh nothing, just you know, um—"

"Relax, Chase. I'm just making conversation," she says.

Chase chugs a throat full of cool ginger beer. He hopes the spicy root punch will punt his anxiety into the stands. Evelyn takes lead.

"Let's start by telling each other about ourselves. You're a college professor right?"

Chase proceeds to talk about his job, his students and Devantay. But doesn't mention Jenae. When Evelyn reciprocates they discover a shared passion for health and fitness. She's a personal trainer. There's a natural ebb and flow to their communication. They vibe well. They grow comfortable with one another. They do all of the unnecessary taps and touches people do when flirting. It leads to a tickle fight.

Evelyn straddles Chase on the sofa. She pokes and prods her fingers along his ribs. As Chase laughs and squirms in the chair she presses her bosom against his torso.

"Well ride 'em cowgirl," Andrea says as she swings an imaginary lasso with one hand and balances a tray of hors d'oeuvres in the other.

"Finger a lady? I mean-*HICCUP*-Lady Fingers anyone?"

"Behave yourself, Andrea. What took you so long?" Chase says.

"Boy, I am not your child. Here…stick a finger in your mouth."

Andrea shoves one of the hors d'oeuvres between Chase's cheeks. She almost teeters over. Evelyn laughs.

"Andrea it's so cool how you two have remained such good friends. I'd be feeling a certain kind of way if some woman was grinding on top of my ex...and in my own house?"

"Girl, th-this ain't nothing. He once had the nerve to get on one knee and propose to a bitch in my house. Right on that spot th-th-there," Andrea wobbles.

"Wow...that's gangsta," Evelyn says.

"No, it's not like that," Chase says.

"Look at him getting all sensitive, Evelyn."

"Awww, she's just messing with you, Chase. Come here."

Evelyn storms into his mouth with her juicy lips. Her kiss is aggressive, commanding and voracious. She has a thick tongue that fills his cheeks. It surprises Chase with its length. The tip of it rings the bell of his tonsils. Andrea clears her throat.

"Hellooo? I cleaned my bedroom for a reason," she says.

Evelyn releases her lip lock and slinks towards Andrea's bedroom.

"You coming?" she says.

"Uh...just give me a minute," he replies.

"Okay. Don't take too long sexy man."

Chase sits up in his chair, elbows on knees, and fingers rubbing his scalp.

"Andrea, this is really going to happen isn't it?"

"Uh....duh," she says.

"You know I'm only doing this because—"

"Yeah, yeah, yeah. Eugene, Eugene, Eugene. Poor wittle Chase. Boo hoo hoo."

"I don't need to listen to your inebriated ass, you know."

"Negro, please."

"Negro?"

"Yeah, *Negro*. Don't get frosty because the white girl you was screwing for three years just got black on you."

Chase opens his mouth to protest.

"Hush. Now go."

Andrea puts her hand on her hip and points down the hall.

Chase sucks his teeth and walks into the bedroom. Candles flicker with the scent of smoked patchouli. The oak fan blows a gentle breeze. Andrea's cranberry and gold comforter has been turned down. The faucet is running in the master bath. Chase sits on the edge of the mattress waiting for Evelyn.

Okay…just be Bob. Be an actor. Play the role. Don't wuss out.

Moments later the faucet shuts and the bathroom door creaks open. The five foot and a li'l bit steps onto the ivory alpaca. She has changed into a sheer black bra, thong, garter with straps and black stockings. Andrea has cued a song from her playlist. She purposefully selected Dawn Penn's *You Don't Love Me*. The same sensual reggae he and Jenae danced to after he proposed. Evelyn private dances for Chase. Her cocoa brown hips twist and shout as she winds up her waist. She slinks over. Chase reaches for her posterior. She smacks his hand and waves a *no-no-no* finger.

Evelyn controls the action. She pushes Chase down and grinds on top. But as she does so there's a clang in the kitchen. Chase ignores it. She slides her hands down his chest and puts her mouth on the bulge of his jeans. She slowly unzips his denims with her teeth. Chase quivers. The thickness in his black jockeys throbs. She puts her lips on him. His arousal is more than he can stand. He slaps his palms on the exposed cheeks of her thong and takes control. They tongue all in and over each other's mouths. Limbs grab and pull in a sensual frenzy

As they tug on the final barriers of their clothing an argument emanates from the kitchen. Angry voices mount. Footsteps approach louder and louder. A furious stomp comes near until…

BOOM

The bedroom door flings open. A startled Chase jumps off of Evelyn. She shrieks. The bright light from the hall temporarily blinds them. Chase can only make out Andrea's long red waves blocking the doorway. But next to her is a stumpy figure that barely reaches her shoulder. Chase squints for his eyes to adjust.

"Bitch, I know what I said. I changed my fucking mind."

"I ain't your bitch and you can't go busting in my bedroom."

Chase's vision clears. Standing next to Andrea is short, pudgy woman he's laid eyes on before.

Evelyn sits up. Her naked brown orbs shine with sweat and saliva.

"Listen here. Ain't shit going down without me being up in here," the stocky woman says.

The woman glares at Chase. She's in a green Philadelphia Eagles hoodie, suede construction boots and baggy cargo shorts. The shorts slouch off of her rear. They reveal plaid boxers wedged tight in the butt crack.

"Andrea, What is this?" Chase asks.

"Kabeerah, you're supposed to be in the other room," Evelyn says.

"You know this person?" Chase says.

"She was *supposed* to stay with me in the pantry," Andrea says, leering at Kabeerah.

"Don't side-eye me white girl. I don't have to stay no goddamn where. I go where my woman goes," Kabeerah says.

"Excuse me? Your woman?" Chase says. He turns to Evelyn. "You're gay?"

"You got a problem with that, Mandingo?" Kabeerah says.

She steps to Chase. Andrea intervenes.

"Bitch, I know you not touching my shoulder right now," Kabeerah says.

Andrea removes her prickly fingers from Kabeerah's sleeve.

"Let's all just settle down, okay?" Andrea says.

"Why is this woman here Andrea?" Chase says.

"This *woman* is *her* woman," Kabeerah says, with a screw face directed at Chase.

"This can't be happening," Chase says.

"Okay, listen Chase. Kabeerah and Evelyn are sorta kinda a couple, yes."

"Sorta kinda?" Kabeerah says.

"It's only natural they would want to…you know…*share* in the experience," Andrea says.

"Share? What is this? A surprise threesome?" Chase says.

"Threesome? Ha. You got the wrong kind of plumbing homeboy," Kabeerah scoffs.

"I can't believe you, Andrea. Really?" Chase says.

He grabs his jeans from around his ankles, hurries them up his legs and zips.

"Chase. They're looking to start a family. I knew you wouldn't be down with a multiple partner experience so I—"

Kabeerah rolls her neck.

"Me neither. Let's be clear," she says.

"So I told Kabeerah she could sit *in the kitchen* with me and watch on the camera," Andrea says.

"Which we *all* agreed to," Evelyn says to Kabeerah.

"I love how *we* didn't include *me*," Chase says. He cuts his eyes at Evelyn.

"Oh, I know you didn't just ice grill my girl," Kabeerah says.

Evelyn jumps between Chase and her hot-headed lover.

"Baby, we talked about this right?" Evelyn says.

She cozies her naked bosom up to her husky lover. Evelyn strokes the teardrop tattoo on Kabeerah's temple. She kisses the prickly stubble of the woman's mohawk. Kabeerah's face softens as she ogles Evelyn's cleavage and licks her earthy lips.

"Now, come on big mama. We agreed. Chase would help us make *our* baby. Yours and mine. No strange clinic. No anonymous donor. We could tell our child that we actually knew their father. That they were conceived in loving passion and not in a test tube. It's what we decided, right baby?"

Evelyn's youthful tone is seductive and innocent. Kabeerah closes her forehead onto Evelyn's skull and nods.

"But why he gotta be all *into* you like that? He's getting you all hot and shit like I do," Kabeerah says.

"Babe, he's a man. They need the proper motivation. Money isn't enough. You know a man ain't nuthin' but a grown up boy. They need that ego boost. That's all I was doing big mama. Boosting his ego."

Evelyn wraps her arms around Kabeerah. Kabeerah grips Evelyn's afro with both hands and tongues her down.

She turns to Chase.

"You know Mr. Chase, you lucky you got high marks on your mental and physical, you feel me? We put a lot of thought into this conception thing. Don't want no ugly, scrawny or unstable kid. If he grow up looking like you I guess that'll work."

"Great. I passed the angry lesbian gangster test," Chase snaps.

"What? Don't make me—"

"Babe, babe it's cool. Remember. Task at hand?" Evelyn says. Kabeerah nods.

"Oookay. Now that that's settled let's all get back to business."

"Okay, but I'm staying," Kabeerah says.

"Yes, of course. We'll go right back in the kitchen where you can monitor the two of—"

"No, I'm staying right here. Right in that ugly ass chair," she says.

"Ugly ass ch—? I'll have you know that's a George Nelson limited ed—"

"Forget the chair, Andrea. This nutcase has nothing to do with this. This was supposed to be a one-on-one thing."

"Nutcase? Let me tell you something. That baby is mine too. And I see I need to take a more *active* role in this shit. Don't worry. I ain't trying to have no man touch me. I'm here to give the baby my vibes, my energy. Karma, Buddha and all that yoga shit…feel me?"

She plops herself in the chair, arms crossed.

Evelyn shrugs, turns her back towards Chase, and winds her rump. The slow drone of the dancehall bass circulates through her hips and her arms. Kabeerah man-spreads in the chair, licks her chocolate jowls and gets ready for the show.

"Hey carrot top. You got anymore of that ginger beer," Kabeerah says.

"Oh *hell* no," Chase says. He shuts off the music.

"Chase what are you doing? Relax. It's all settled," Evelyn says.

"Settled? You honestly expect us to have sex in front of your gay lover?"

Kabeerah jumps out of the chair and barrels toward Chase.

"Oh, so is that what this is? You a homophobe now?" she says.

"A homophobe? What? No. I just—"

"Then why I gotta be a *gay* lover huh? Why can't I just be a lover?" Kabeerah bumps her chest into Chase.

"You better back up off of me lady," Chase says.

Kabeerah turns her nose up. She scans Chase up and down like he's short.

"This be-yatch here. I'm glad you didn't stick your little fairy ass wee wee up in my girl. We'd have to raise a little bitch boy like his bitch daddy. Is that your problem? You a little punk ass bitch?"

Kabeerah pokes her index finger in Chase's temple. Chase's natural reflex is to slap her hand away. As he does so she stumbles backward, trips over Evelyn's sneaker, and falls on her butt. Chase tries to apologize.

"I'm sorry. I didn't mean for you to fall like that."

Kabeerah squints, squares up and leaps. She winds up and hurls her fist forward.

POW!

She lands a solid right hook on Chase's left cheek. He falls backward onto the mattress. Kabeerah pounces on top of him and starts to pummel his face.

"You wanna take it to the streets? We from Philly. Show you how we do."

Kabeerah is relentless. She unleashes a barrage of blows.

"Philly, my nigga…[she punches]….This how we do. Phillaaay, Niggaaa," she screams.

Chase tries to lock her wrists. It's against his moral compass to strike back at her. Andrea stands petrified in the doorway.

"Andrea don't just stand there," Chase yells. "Andrea?"

Chase secures Kabeerah wrists so she resorts to something else.

"Argh," Chase yells in pain. He looks down to see Kabeerah gnawing on his shoulder

"Philly, nigga. We fight dirty, my nigga," she screams.

Andrea finally shakes off her shocked stupor. She rushes over and rips Kabeerah off of Chase.

"Oh, okay white girl. You want some of this too?"

"Baby. Baby wait," Evelyn says. "Let's all just calm down. We can still harness all this energy for the baby."

Kabeerah lunges at Chase again. But he's prepared for her this time. Chase bobs and weaves before putting her in a headlock.

"Evelyn grab your bag. Everying….Come on chop, chop."

Evelyn does as asked.

Kabeerah tries to jostle out of Chase's grip. His muscular arms keep her subdued as he drags her out of the bedroom.

"Andrea get the front door," he says.

Andrea opens the door. The elevator is waiting. A barefoot Evelyn, now wearing Chase's shirt, tosses her clothes inside.

"I'm so sorry about this Chase. For what it's worth you would've made a great donor," she says. She jumps up and kisses Chase's cheek as he continues struggling with Kabeerah.

"Get off. Let me go goddammit. Philly my nigga."

Evelyn scoots inside the elevator. Andrea presses the lobby button. Chase and Andrea eyeball each other. Chase counts off.

"A one…a two…a three."

He flings the enraged woman into the elevator. Before she can recover Andrea slams the gate and sends the elevator down. They walk back in the apartment.

"Chase I—"

"Shhh. Don't you say a word. Not one. Single. Word."

He feels the scratches on his chest. And winces from the throbbing in his shoulder. He grabs his overcoat and walks out.

"Chase wait. You're not even wearing a shirt."

He slams the door and takes the stairs down. As he steps into the chill of a winter's night he thinks of his tension filled day and maniacal night. He wonders if things could get any worse. He won't have to wonder for long. He's about to receive a very special phone call.

11 Mister Telephone Man

✻

Chase sucks hot steam through the cones of his nostrils. He opens his jaw, closes, spits and repeats. The childlike action is calming. Bathroom mist wafts into the bedroom and over the mattress like a stretched cotton. The bed is only half-made. His side is rumpled. Hers is smooth. As he shuts off the shower the doorbell rings.

"Hey babe, can you get that? That should be Devantay." He waits for confirmation. The doorbell rings again.

"Babe…Hey Babe!"

"I heard you the first time," Jenae yells from the first floor.

Her voice is monotone—as if spoken into her chest. After ten minutes the fresh and clean Chase bounds downstairs.

"Nah, Miss Jenae. The Hulk is human like us but when he gets mad he metamamorphisizes into—"

"Metamamorphisizes?" Jenae says, with a curious smile.

"Uh huh. He changes into a mutant beast. And check it out. He can beat anybody. I mean *anybody*," Devantay says.

"Sounds impressive," Jenae says.

"And then he'll start running and go Hulk smash. Hulk smash." Devantay stomps around the living room which amuses Jenae.

"Well, there's my lady's smile," Chase says.

Jenae glances at him. Her smile dissolves.

"Anyway. Devantay, the word is actually metamorphosize. It's a verb from the noun metamorphosis. But a better choice of words, because it flows better, would be to say he *morphs* into a mutant. Morph is when something—or someone [she glances at Chase]—

changes so much that he—I mean *it*—turns into something you've never seen before," she says.

"Wow. I bet you know all the comic book characters," Devantay says.

"Oh, I know about characters all right," she says.

Chase walks over to Devantay and rubs the preteen's bushy head.

"Boy, we're going to have to stop at Kitchen Kutz before the game this afternoon. That 'fro is a mess," Chase says.

"Stop Chase. You gonna mess up my hair," Devantay says.

"You can't mess up what's already a mess. Right babe?" Chase says.

Jenae keeps her vintage horn rimmed glasses buried in the computer screen on her lap.

"Hey Chase, can I raid the fridge?" he says.

Chase nods. Devantay scampers into the kitchen. Jenae leans back against the sofa's armrest. Her outstretched legs take up the length of the two seater. Chase has to sit on the edge of the coffee table instead.

"So…what you working on?" he says.

"Work."

"Okay, Jenae what's going on? What's the deal?"

"Nothing. I have a lot of work to do."

"So is that why your side of the bed was still made? You slept on the couch doing work?"

Her fingers rocket like a receptionist on the keyboard.

"Babe, I asked you a question. What's wrong?"

"No, I didn't come to bed alright? I slept on the couch."

"Yes, but Babe, why? You've been a bit…*off* lately."

"*I've* been off?"

"I mean, *we*. I should have said *we've* been off lately. Sweetheart listen. I've been dealing with alot at work recently. And I just want to tell you that I…that I…."

Chase hesitates as he notices Jenae is no longer paying attention. She lasers in on his shoulder, leaps from the sofa and tugs the shoulder strap of his ribbed tank aside.

"What the…what the *fuck* is that?" she says.

The rare F bomb takes Chase aback. She gives little time for his response.

"Is that a fucking bite mark?" she says.

"Huh? A what?"

Chase bolts to the cherrywood mirror above the mantle. There's a small red splotch with two rows of indentations on his skin. It's as if he's been bitten by a monster baby. He pokes and prods his shoulder with a series of—manufactured—perplexed facial expressions. He's stalling. Chase knows full well where that bite mark came from. *Damn psycho, Philly freak.* He needs an excuse. And fast. Jenae's reflection is seething in the mirror.

"Are you kidding me? Really?" Chase sucks his teeth. "Can you believe this shit? Wild ass kids. Unbelievable."

"Kids?" Jenae squints an eye.

"Devantay. Hey Devantay get in here."

Jenae's expression turns quizzical. The young boy scurries back with an open bottle of Reed's Ginger Beer.

"Yeah? What's up Chase?" he says.

"Look at this. You see this?" Chase points to the surface wound.

"Dayyum yo. What the hell? I mean heck," he says.

"That kid must have bit me yesterday. You know, the pudgy one? The one I had to hold back during the fight?" Chase says.

Devantay's left eye shrivels for a moment before quickly returning to normal. Chase continues the fabrication.

"What was his name again?" Chase starts snapping his fingers and hopes beyond hope that Devantay's street smarts kick in.

"You got into a fight Devantay?" Jenae says.

Devantay pauses. Chase swallows.

"Yeah, Miss Jenae. It was crazy. See these three dudes jumped me at the group home yesterday—"

Chase jumps in.

"I forgot I had a mentors meeting at the group home before I linked up with Tanaka in Hamptons."

"Shush. Let *him* tell the story. Go ahead, Devantay."

"So yeah, right in the middle of Chase's meeting. These dudes was saying how I think I'm better than them because my mentor be takin' me to all these dope places and he do real shit with me. But they mentors is just a bunch of bum bitches. But Chase really be caring and shit. So they jumped me. But I punched the one guy in the nose. Knocked him right on his fat ass."

Devantay relishes the opportunity to cuss and use slang knowing Chase wouldn't dare admonish him.

Jenae puts her hand on Devantay's shoulder.

"Were you hurt?" she says.

"Nah, I'm good. Chase heard everything. But I was like, *bam* punch in the face, then *boom* knee in the gut, I was Iron Man taking on those two punk bitches… I mean three punk bi—"

Chase senses the excited child is about to get carried away and sabotage the story. He interjects.

"—So I got between Devantay and the other kids. One of them tripped me and I fell to the floor. That's when the pudgy kid…umm what's his name again, Devantay? You mentioned him once before?"

"Cake. That's when Cake jumped on top of Chase and bit him in the neck…I mean his shoulder," Devantay says.

BEEP BEEP BEEP

Jenae's cell phone rings.

"Hmmm. Well, I'm just glad you're okay. But do your best to avoid fights next time. Especially against three guys, little junior Hulk," she says. She answers and takes the call in the kitchen.

Chase watches her disappear and then leans over to Devantay.

"Well, you're pretty quick on your feet aren't you?"

"It only took a sec to see you needed me to lie. You learn fast in group."

He takes a swig of the ginger beer.

"Listen D-man. It wasn't good that I lied. And it really wasn't good for you to lie too."

"Oh okay. You want me to tell Miss Jenae I lied? I mean you never even came by yesterday."

"Shh, shh, no of course not. I just don't want you to think that was cool. It was just something that I kind of...*had* to do."

"Come on Chase. I get it. You're a playa. You was getting your mack on. Word that's dope."

"No, Devantay. Being a player is not *dope* and 'm not macking. How do you even know that word?"

Devantay stink-eyes Chase.

"Alright I get it. You're no dummy. We'll talk about it later."

"So, who bit you?"

"I can't say right now...wait...you hear that?...Is Jenae yelling?"

Jenae's voice crescendos as she storms back in, clutching her cell.

"For the third time who is this? How'd you get this number?"

Devantay and Chase gawk at Jenae, confused.

"Yes, he's bald. About six foot two. 6' 3" to be exact. Yes, he lives in a brownstone but I'm not about to answer a bunch of—Excuse me?"

Jenae's light brown complexion morphs into fire.

"Who are you talking t—" Chase asks.

Jenae puts her palm up. Devantay sits on the edge of the couch, nursing his soda.

"Yes, he's a professor. With *you* last weekend? Who is this? Who? Tevarus' wife? Who the hell is Tevarus?"

Chase's heart thuds against his sternum. His veins pulse and pop with fear. That name. Tevarus. He never expected to hear it again. A lump forms in his throat.

"*Who* is on the phone, Jenae?" Chase demands.

Jenae's hands tremble. Her eyes pool. She puts the phone on speaker. A heavily accented Dominican woman speaks:

"Joo listen to me. I no know what he tell you but he name is Tay-Vah-Rus. We marry in Bawston."

Jenae composes herself.

"Boston? How long ago in Boston?" Jenae says, knowing that Chase has always claimed to be from Boston.

"Seven year ago. We marry as kids. We only eighteen, nineteen year old. Cuando mi abuela morió...when my grandmother died. I visit mi familía in The Dominican Republic and transfer the money she left for me to our bank account. But when I come back he no here. He clean out all the money, mamí. Todos. All this time I look for him. Den I hear from somebody, that he a teacher in Nueva York en una escuela. At a college. I track him down three week ago. We meet. He apologize and everything. Then he take me back to he place in Brooklyn and I spend the night."

"Wait, wait. You're telling me that *my* man brought you back here when I was away last weekend? This can't be happening."

"Jenae, I have no idea who this woman—"

"Shut up." Jenae *pistol-points* at his nose.

"Listen mama. I no care about you being his girlfriend. I his wife you understand me, sí? Tevarus say he need sum time to figure out dis and dat. I gave him his time. Pero he no call me back for tres semanas. That's three weeks. So now I call you."

"This can't be happening," Jenae says. She rakes her fingers through her hair and rolls her eyes to the ceiling. "How did you get my number?"

Chase tries to speak.

"Jenae look she—"

"Shut up, I said."

Devantay sits on the edge of his seat, glued to the drama.

"When he fall sleep I go through he phone. He no have no passcode on the phone, tú sabes?"

"Yeah I *sabes*. You're right he doesn't use a code," Jenae says.

"I look the call history. A Jenny numero keep coming up. Jenny, Jenny, Jenny so I put two and two together. You understanded me?"

"Oh, I understand you, alright," Jenae says.

Chase whispers, "But your name is Jenae not Jenny."

Jenae puts the phone on mute.

"I said shut it. She has an accent. You know she means Jenae when she says, Jenny."

Jenae unmutes.

"Listen, I have known Chase for years," Jenae says.

"Chay? Who Chay? He name is Tevarus. He tell you it's Chay?"

"Now, I'm all confused. You're telling me that my man is already married and his name is Tevarus?"

Jenae clutches her curls and paces the room. Chase is helpless. Devantay looks on as if he wishes he had a bag of popcorn.

"Jenae she's lying," is the best Chase can muster.

"She knows your height, features, job, you live in a brownstone, you're from Boston, how could you do this?" Jenae says, fighting sniffles and teardrops.

"How you *not* know he married mama? My name tattoo right on he culo…Damaris. It's right there. Don't play estupido."

"Tattoo?" Jenae says.

Jenae knows that Chase despises tattoos. It was their first and only real argument until their recent troubles. Jenae wanted to get a scales of justice and a cap and tassels logo on her ankle. It was to signify their careers. Chase said no. Jenae felt that Chase was being controlling. He still won't say why he hates tattoos.

"Chase doesn't have a tattoo," Jenae says.

"Mamí please. It's right on his ass okay?"

"I told you he doesn't have a goddamn tattoo. But wait. You said you were here, right. Describe this house."

"It's not a house mama. He live in a brownstone apartment building. Seventeen floor. 17B. B, like boy."

"That's not what a brownstone is Je—"Chase says.

"Hush," Jenae says. She returns to the woman on the call.

"And what about the college. Which one does he work at?"

"Long Island University in downtown Brooklyn."

Chase sits down next to Devantay and breathes easier.

"And you got my number from his phone you say?"

"Sí."

"What's the number?"

"What's the number? I just dialed it, mama."

"I know, I know. Just repeat it to me please."

The woman rattles off ten numbers. Devantay laughs.

"Ha, you dumb. That ain't Miss Jenae number," Devantay says.

Chase gives a relieved half-smile.

"That's not my number. It's close. You misdialed."

"No, no, no. His name is Tevarus and he—"

"Okay, we went through that. But just to be sure…do this. You have a pic of him right?"

"Sí, claro. Of course I do. Yo tengo."

Chase fidgets in his seat.

"Text it to me. The number you actually dialed," Jenae says.

"Okay, un momento."

Thirty seconds pass. It is the longest half-minute of Chase's Brooklyn life. Two quick vibrations on Jenae's phone alert her to an incoming text. Jenae taps the screen. Her eyebrows raise and her mouth smirks. A sigh of relief replaces her fury.

"Well your Tevarus is certainly not my Chase. Same bald head but I guess I should have confirmed that we were both talking about a Black man at least."

"He Black? Oh no, no. Tevarus es chino. Ay Díos. Lo siento. I am so sorry, Jenny."

"It's okay. I hope things work out with your husband. Goodbye."

The conversation is finally over. Jenae's face is flushed. She dries the trickles on her cheekbones. Chase rushes to embrace her. Jenae buries her face in the valley of his chest.

"Babe I'm so sorry," she says.

Chase strokes her hair and kisses her forehead.

"I can't believe I let some wrong number, and a crazy story, get me all flustered like this," she says.

"Sweetheart it's okay. I made you feel like you had something to worry about. Any woman would have done the same thing."

"No, it's not okay. I don't know what's wrong with me. I've never been that crazy, jealous, insecure chick."

"I know. And that's why I'm marrying you," Chase says. He wraps his arm around her waist. Jenae clutches the back of his scalp like a bowling ball. They stab their tongues and slop their lips.

"Yuck. Hello? Impressionable preteen here," Devantay waves. "This is gross. I'm going to make a sandwich." He scamps into the kitchen.

BUZZ BUZZ BUZZ

"Hmmm, is that a phone in your pocket or...*ahem, ahem*?" Jenae says, with a wry smile.

Chase returns a devilish grin and squeezes her curves.

"Go answer your phone frisky man. I'm going to hop in the shower. You might want to make that call a quick one," she winks.

Jenae slips from his grasp and jogs upstairs. Chase breathes an uneasy sigh. He wonders how many bullets he can keep dodging without taking one to the chest. He looks at the number on the screen:

INCOMING CALL

PRIVATE NUMBER

"Hello?" Chase answers.

"Well, hello there Tevarus."

The familiar voice makes him crush the receiver.

"Eugene," Chase says.

"Well how are you Tevarus?"

"Stop calling me that."

"Why Papi? You no like? Huh, Papi Chulo?" Eugene cackles.

Chase cradles the phone to his mouth and walks to the far corner of the living room.

"Eugene. What the hell were you thinking calling Jenae?"

"Well, technically *I* didn't call her. That was a very well compensated associate of mine. I think she deserves an academy award for that performance don't you? And peep this. She ain't even Dominican. African-American actor chick I know. Narrates audio books and shit. Owed me a favor."

"We had an agreement Eugene."

"Yeah, playboy. But your slow rolling and fuckups ain't payin' the bills. Why I had to get a call from a fat dike on a temper tantrum?"

"That wasn't my fault. What the hell Eugene? You set me up with *two* women? Lesbians at that?"

"You can thank your redhead bunny rabbit for that one. She suggested lesbians. Said they be the low hanging fruit for this sort of thing. It's the only thing they actually *need* a man for," he laughs.

"Is this some sick joke to you Eugene?"

"Don't act like a bitter bitch. You act like you don't get anything out this deal"

"I don't. If you think sex is an incentive then you do it? I *have* a woman. A great woman. And you almost blew up my spot if she didn't have a lawyer's brain. She asked the right questions to your fake Dominican."

"Sex ain't no incentive? Really? So your chumpy didn't get hard last night?"

"Is that all you can think about?"

"Stop being a prissy sissy. I was only going to let that phone call go but so far. I didn't even give her all your correct information did I? I could have told her your full government name, Tevarus Huxley. And how you were this high school football prospect from Georgia. And how your ass ain't never even *been* to Boston. But I didn't do that, did I?"

"Lucky for me you didn't. Jenae is smart. She's a lawyer for crying out loud. A damn good one. All she needs is a full name. She's a bulldog. And a bulldog in a pretty dress is still a bulldog."

"Don't worry about Jenae. Bam got your sweet ass this far didn't he? You don't even have a real degree but look how you about to run a department. So keep your end of the bargain or everything you love goes abracadabra. Including that hot piece of tail lawyer."

"I'm trying. These women are crazy. Some European fetish chick that wants a biracial kid as a trophy. And then you give me the anger management lesbians?"

"Check it…we're not unreasonable. The call to Jenae was Bam's idea. He said you needed a reminder. A wake-up call. You woke?"

Chase doesn't respond.

"I'll that as a yes. Now this next one is your last chance. This chick is perfect. She's not crazy. She's *very* heterosexual. Educated, calm, cool, collected type. And she's fine as a mofo. I'd smash it fo' sho'."

"We already know what *your* priorities are. But what sort of vetting did you do? That means—"

"I know what the fuck *vetting* means, nigga. I ain't stupid. Anyway, the best vetting you can get. She's Man-Man's cousin."

Chase drops the phone to his side and slaps the heel of his palm on his forehead.

"Your goon's cousin is the next date? *That's* who you picked?"

"I *vetted* her myself. She understands the deal. She ain't looking for nothing but a smart, healthy child with good genes. And she's paying *double* what we been asking. Chick got it like that. Some kind of artist I think."

"You *think*? You didn't vet a damn thing," Chase says. He hears the shower turn off and Jenae's footsteps exit the bathroom upstairs. "Look, I gotta go."

"That's cool playboy. We done for now anyway. The white bitch got your instructions for this. And Chase?"

"What, Eugene?"

"Don't fuck this one up. My next call won't be some actress."

12 Rayne Chimes

❧

His gaze fights the wind and snow. His palms sting and tremble. *Why don't I ever buy gloves?* He flicks the flakes from the screen and follows the blue dot on the GPS. He sloshes across Sixth Avenue and peers up. *Leroy Street? I hate when Manhattan streets have names. Who ever heard of a Leroy Street?*

The beauty of navigating Manhattan is the city's grid system. Sweet simplicity. Streets go east and west. Avenues, north and south. Both with commonsense sequential numbers. But when it comes to those named streets? They confound even the most seasoned New Yorker. Chase is trying to find a certain West Village coffeehouse. *Damn thing says I'm standing right here. But I don't see an Asha Café.* He scans and he scours. Snow-caked stoops. A tattoo parlor to his rear. And a nightclub down the street advertising their *Boys with Toys* all-male revue.

"Chase. Chase, come on already it's freezing."

The voice comes from behind and below. It's Andrea.

Chase pivots and peers down. Andrea calls from steps that lead slightly below street level. Like many Manhattan businesses, the Asha Café is nestled below the sidewalk—under the tattoo parlor. Chase follows her. He hesitates to stomp the snow off of his caribou winter boots. Coffee sipping faces grimace at the windy door being held open for him.

"Chase," Andrea bellows.

Chase squeezes through the tight aisle between the coffee bar and tables. The brick walls are decorated with New York City themed photography. The famous *Tribute in Light of 9/11* hangs beside a print of underground subway musicians. Chase admires the art and savors the aroma of overpriced espresso.

"Hey. You're not for the ambiance. Sit," Andrea says.

"I'm not a puppy, Andrea."

Chase sits in the open chair across from her. He removes his skull cap and starts to unbutton his coat.

"Don't bother, you're not going to be here long enough," she says.

A cheery barista bounces to their table.

"Hey guys. I'm Carrie. Can I get you a—"

"No. He won't be here that long," Andrea says, with a dismissive wave.

"Don't be rude, Andrea. Forget her Carrie. Yes, I'd like a—"

"Chase you don't have time."

"For a cup of coffee? Seriously, Andrea?"

"I'll speak slower…You. Don't. Have. Time."

"Ummm, I think I'll just come back later," Carrie says.

"Don't look at me like that, Chase. Eugene didn't have me text you for coffee and convo."

"Glad you brought him up. We need to get something straight. I don't like how you're involved in this. And I don't like this cozy relationship you seem to have with Eugene."

"Why? You jealous?"

"Of course not. And your cat and mouse games aren't cute."

"Here," Andrea says.

She reaches inside her oversized Coach bag and pulls out a furry teddy bear. It is costumed in a spiked leather collar and faux leather undies. Attached to its paws are a pair of tiny plastic handcuffs. Chase returns a confused stare.

"It's not for you. It's to give to your date, Rayne. Rayne Chimes."

"Gift? Why would why I—wait…what? Her name is Rain?"

"Yes, spelled R-A-Y-N-E Chimes. Like wind chimes. She'll explain it."

"Okay, whatever. And not that I don't appreciate the idea of a gift but isn't giving a grown woman a stuffed animal kind of, uh… middle school?"

"It's not a *gift* gift. More of a trojan horse."

"Trojan horse?"

"Mmmhmm. Look at the face."

Chase scrutinizes. He shakes and shrugs.

"Don't just look. *Inspect*. The eyes."

Chase lasers in on the plastic eyelets of the teddy.

"Is that…is that a camera?" he asks.

"It's a nanny cam," she says, with an eyebrow-pop of pride.

"A nanny cam? Why would…ohhhhh. The video. That's right. We're not in your apartment this time."

"I live in a loft not an apartment."

"Really?"

"The distinction is important. Anyway. Since I won't be in Rayne's apartment to monitor the action, I went to a spy shop downtown. I explained what I wanted to do, and the creepy guy hooked me up with this."

"But how does it—"

"—work? It's ingenious. The Wi-Fi is in the ear. I've already activated it. It will transmit the video to an app on my phone. I can watch, record, turn off, turn on, all from my phone. And the spiked collar? That middle spike? That's the microphone."

"Damn. This is some serious *Mission Impossible* stuff right here."

"Now don't mess up. Make sure the bear can see you. Don't leave it in another room. And keep your wits about you. Don't get all hot 'n heavy and lose focus because you got aroused…like last time."

"Like last ti—? Whatever, anything else Sherlock?"

"No. Here. Put it in this gift bag I bought. You know where you're going right?"

"Yeah, yeah. It's in my GPS. Couple of blocks from here."

Andrea's face is expressionless. Chase waits for her to speak.

"What?…Bye!" she says.

"Drama queen," he mumbles.

He shoehorns his way through the coffee crowd and back to the cold. The steady snowfall quiets the city. He battles the wind gusts and crunches the frosty flakes. After a few minutes he arrives at a three story apartment building. He buzzes 2A. He bounces for warmth and huffs hot breaths into the cradle of his palms. He doesn't have to shiver for long as the intercom on the steel panel crackles with a voice.

"Who is it?"

"Hi. Rayne?"

"That be me," she says.

"It's Chase."

"Okay, I'll buzz you. Second floor. Make a right for 2A.

The metal door unlocks with a click and a long buzz. He stomps the snow as he enters, walks up the stairs and raps on her door.

Chase hears the approach of footsteps rising above mid-tempo Jazz. He decides to be playful and cover the peephole with his palm.

"Haha, very funny mister," she replies.

"You don't get to decide if I'm handsome enough to let in," Chase says.

"Too late. I've already seen several pictures," she says.

She unlocks the deadbolt and slides the door chain. It creaks open partway.

"You have to step inside all the way so I can close the door behind you. I have the typical tight Manhattan hallway," she says. Chase steps into the candle lit corridor.

"Let me take your coat," she says.

Chase gets his first look at her. *Wow*, he says to himself.

Rayne is a striking, natural beauty. Her almond skin is flawless. Her moist tresses spring into a bushel of twists that curve around her cheekbones. They bring out the fullness of lips that are more juicy than pouty. And even without make-up her face is vibrant. She's of average height for a woman. Her copper crown crests at Chase's lip. The apartment is toasty enough for her to greet him in an ankle-length, bohemian summer dress. Chase extends his hand. She brushes it aside and hugs him instead.

"Peace and blessings of the universe," she says.

She nooses her elbows around his broad shoulders for a chest-to-bosom embrace. Rayne gives the kind of hug most people don't share with strangers. It has the coziness of a lover, or a friend with benefits.

"Mmmm, you give nice hugs, Chase."

"You're not so bad yourself, Rayne."

Although she is neither supermodel thin, nor video vixen thick, Chase can feel her hidden curves. They linger their embrace before she slides her arms to links their palms. She leads him into the belly of the apartment.

The square living room sparkles with polished parquet floors and wall art. A dozen fine art photos deck the walls. They are all candids of indigenous women and girls. Happy. At peace. At play. Dancing, hugging…simply enjoying life.

"I hope you don't mind not having any furniture to sit on. I live a minimalist lifestyle. It's better for my chi. Clutter is chaos. Open space is peace."

"No, the floor cushions will be just fine," he says and eyes the photos. "These pictures are amazing. The emotion, the landscapes, beautiful."

"I'll take that as a compliment," she says.

"You're the photographer?"

"It's how I pay for these Greenwich Village digs."

"I notice your subjects are all female," he says.

"I wanted to capture women with other women. Show sisterhood, motherhood, friendship. But without the male presence."

It is at this point that Chase notices how Rayne speaks the way a songbird sings. She has a melodic tone to her voice which puts him at ease.

"So, I have to ask. Is Rayne Chimes your real name? It's so unique."

"Yes, my Dad gave me the name. My mom couldn't stop her tears of joy when I was born. It was like rain. And Dad said my laughter was like the giggle of wind chimes. Put them together and voila."

"Great story. Oh, by the way this is for you."

Chase presents the gift bag.

"A present? Ooh goodie goodie," she says, with a clap and a jig. She removes the teddy. She stiff-arms it in the air and twists her face.

"Oh…okay. A uh…stuffed animal?" She forces a smile.

"You don't like it, do you?"

"No, no it's not that. It's just. Well, I haven't had a guy give me one of these since I was…I don't know…twelve?"

Damned Andrea, he says to himself. Chase puts it in the corner.

"Don't be mad. It's sweet and it's positive. You're sweet. I know the perfect place in my room for it. I'll put it there later," she says.

"I hope you like vegan." Rayne guides him into the cozy kitchen. "If you don't, you will tonight. Don't let the pretty face fool ya'. I can throw down."

Rayne opens the oven door and takes out a pan of bubbling lasagna. The aroma of melted soy cheese, tomato and spices invade Chase's nostrils. He hovers over the savory steam.

"Mmmm, succulent," he says.

"Like I told you. I can throw down."

Chase laughs. Her wit and confidence is like a magnet.

"When I say succulent I'm not talking about the food," he says.

"Why, Mister Chase Archibald. Are you flirting with me?"

She brushes a finger down his spine.

Chase notices a large wooden salad bowl next to a pile of leafy greens, deep red plum tomatoes, colossal cucumbers, purple carrots and a container of black olives.

"Rayne, were you making a salad?"

"Oh my goodness, yes. Let me—"

"No. Let me. You set up the plates I'll finish the salad."

Cool points for Chase. Rayne cuts a smile.

After a few minutes dinner is ready to be served. They return to the living room. Rayne lowers the volume on the streaming jazz station. They sit cross-legged on handmade seat cushions. Chase grabs a fork to dig in but Rayne pauses. She bows with cupped hands. After a few seconds she palms her heart. And returns her gaze.

"Had to give thanks to the universe. Okay, let's eat," she says.

Chase stabs a chunky morsel of the vegan pasta and circles it into his mouth. The bold zest of the tomato sauce and the smooth creamy texture of the melted soy mozzarella makes him swoon.

"Mmmm. This is incredible. And vegetarian?"

"Vegan. I'm glad you like it."

They eat, drink and laugh. A soulful connection develops. They vibe on discussions around art and creativity, education and social justice. They converse about books, spirituality and the quest for internal peace. And it is peace that Rayne truly exemplifies. Her stable spirit is soothing to a man whose soul is in turmoil. Chase grabs the music remote and pairs Rayne's bluetooth speakers with his phone.

"Check you out. Just taking over like you runnin' things here."

Chase thumbs through his playlist and selects *Window Seat* by Erykah Badu. The distinctive rat-a-tat-tat of the snare drum intro elicits a smile.

"Mmmm, love this song. Everyone says I remind them of her."

"Eh. A little. She's way more eccentric," Chase says.

He rises from the cushion, and extends his palm.

"May I have this dance?"

Rayne blushes as she steadies herself. Chase hooks her waist and they groove cheek-to-cheek. As Rayne melts in his arms, desire sparks a request.

"Kiss me," she says.

Chase pokes his index finger under her chin and dives in full compliance. Tongues lock and load and slap and slop. Her breaths increase. Soft, supple breasts heave into irocnclad pecs.

"Oh God," she moans as Chase's lips stumble on a pleasure point on her neck. He devours her scent. Rayne's *Egyptian Musk* body oil is intoxicating.

"Damn, you smell good," he whispers.

"Chase, I want you."

Chase smoothes his large palms over her deceptively plump peach bottom. He continues down to the back of her thighs and seizes them. He catapults her legs up. She wraps them around his waist.

"Oh. Strong…such…you are that," she says. Rayne is so aroused she can't form a proper sentence.

Chase slams her back against the wall causing the teddy bear to fall face forward onto the floor. Still clothed, he grinds into her. The moistness between her legs tingles against the firmness between his.

"Oh Chase...off, off...take these off," she says.

They rush to remove their clothes. Chase's pocket vibrates first.

She stands with cleavage bouncing, shoulders bobbing, and lungs panting in a disheveled dress.

"You're not actually checking that are you?" Rayne says.

"I know, mood killer. I'll shut it off. Don't move," Chase says.

He checks the display first:

ANDREA

Chase. What are you doing?

Pick up the damn bear!

I can only see the floor.

Before Chase can sit the bear upright, Rayne stomps over and grabs his wrist. The stuffed animal falls flat on its face again.

"I can give orders to you know. Now kneel."

Chase drops to his knees. Rayne stands over him and seductively peels off her dress and bares her breasts. She points.

"I want another kiss...here...and here," she says.

Chase grabs and suctions each almond mound into his mouth.

"Oh shiiii-Chase...Ch-Ch-Chase."

Chase slides his boxers past his shins. He tugs at the rim of her panties. They cascade to the parquet floor. His phone alerts again but he ignores it as he lays Rayne down and spreads her trembling thighs. His stiffness plops with a thud onto her lush warmth. As he gazes into her eyes she says...

"Wait. Wait. Chase please ummm. Wait."

"Huh? Wh-what do you mean?"

"Chase, I'm sorry...I'm..."

Rayne's cheeks turn red. She shivers. Chase removes his heavy frame from between her and she bolts into the bathroom. He hears her whimper as water streams from the sink. His mind races with competing questions of doubt and fear. *Did I hurt her? Is she scared?* The faucet shuts off. Rayne reemerges, patting her face with a towel.

"Are you okay?" he says in a velvet tone.

Rayne can see the anxiety in his eyes.

"It's not you, Chase."

Her discomfort is obvious. Chase wraps his arms around her. She sinks into security. They lounge on the floor in silence as Chase strokes her hair and kisses her forehead.

"You're smiling now. Why?" he says.

"Because, I'm laying naked with a man I just met and when I get emotional and run he doesn't freak out. He looks at me with his sexy, sensitive eyes and just holds me. Patiently."

Chase continues to comfort her.

"This wasn't supposed to go like this," she says.

He wipes a spindle of her hair from her eye.

"So what happened?"

Rayne bows her head and laughs at herself.

"You're going to think I'm silly and childish," she says.

"Really? I'm the one that gave you a teddy bear."

Rayne chuckles. He glances at the bear to see it lying face down.

"So are you going to tell me?" Chase says.

"Well, it was something you did."

"Damn, I knew it. What did I do wrong?"

"I didn't say you did anything *wrong*, I said it was something you *did*. Well, everything you did. You're strong but tender."

"Sounds good so far," Chase says.

"You made me feel alive. Like someone else used to."

"Someone else?"

Chase turns to face her and weaves their fingers together.

"My boyfriend, or whatever he is right now. He's a musician."

"You have a boyfriend?"

Chase frowns.

"And you have a fiancée," Rayne fires back.

"Touché. Continue," he says.

"His name is Ilyas. We've been in some sort of relationship since we were fifteen. So that's almost twenty years now. We've been friends, cuddle buddies, friends with benefits, boyfriend/girlfriend, everything and *no* thing. He loves me but he's never been committed 100% to *anything* but his music. I've wanted a child for years but the man I love doesn't have the time, or the desire."

"Have you talked about? Shared your feelings?"

"It's one excuse after another. I need to wait for him to get back from tour, now's not the right time, money's tight, or the big one… he's joining some late night talk show's house band in LA so he doesn't have time to be a dad. Then we argue and it ends with how I knew what I was signing up for, he's married to his music blah, blah, blah. But…wait for it…he still *loves* me."

"So why don't you simply leave?"

"Because love is never *simple*. Love is always complicated. You of all people should know that, Chase."

Her comment hits home.

"So do you feel guilty? Being here with me?" he says.

"Guilty? No. I made a decision to do this because I wanted a child. And I wanted a child in the most natural way. You've seen the kind of person I am. I believe in energy. I believe our energy goes into an embryo. And I want to conceive a child with someone I could say I knew. I touched. Whose energy I felt and loved. Even if that love was only for one night. So, no. You didn't do anything wrong, Chase. You just reminded me of love."

And Rayne's comments only remind Chase of Jenae. And of his predicament.

"Honestly, Rayne I don't understand why any woman would want to do have a baby like this. I mean I have *my* reasons but—"

"Chase, have you *tried* to understand? Tried to understand why these women would want to make a baby with you?"

Chase pauses.

"Women aren't like men. You guys can sleep with anyone. Then you can zip up your pants, eat a bologna sandwich, and go have a brew. Women? We want to know the man we are sleeping with. A sperm donor is anonymous. All he does is donate sperm. But you? Chase, you're THE donor. You're someone whose skin we can touch. Whose cologne we can get high on. Whose lips we can devour. Whose intelligence stimulates us. And whose confidence we can feel protected by. Try getting that from a fertility clinic."

Chase nods.

"Even the lesbian ladies that came to you. They wanted a child as a couple. They wanted to share the experience of creating life and wanted a good man like you for the job."

"You knew about them?" Chase asks.

"My cousin Gregory…well you call him Man-Man…he tells me everything. I've *been* up to speed on this whole arrangement between you and Eugene."

"So you know Eugene is forcing me do this. To keep my life in tact."

"Hmmm. I don't know if it's as *forced* as you're making it out to be. You made a choice to be here. And I think you're enjoying us being together right now. But it's your choice, Chase. There are always consequences. There's always a cost. But maybe you just need to stop being afraid of the price."

"I feel like I'm on a couch with Oprah."

"I'm just being a friend," she says.

Rayne's words force Chase to dig into a well of inconvenient truths. Explaining to him why women would want him to be the donor, makes him question his own motivations.

"You've given me a lot to think about."

"And you gave me a safe space to share my feelings. I appreciate you."

They sit and listen to the wintry quiet. The fires of the candlewicks on the kitchen counter cast dancing shadows on the walls. A warm glow flickers on her brown skin. She smiles at her palms.

"Wow, we've been holding hands this whole time?" Rayne says.

"Yes, we have," Chase smiles back.

They stare at each other with looks of longing. Chase massages her delicate fingers. Rayne sits on her knees and licks the sweat of his dome. She pecks his temple and then his cheek. Chase cradles her jaw for a kiss. She blocks his lips with a finger.

"I want to wake up in your arms," she says.

"So you still want to do this?" he replies.

"I didn't say that. Maybe I just want to fall asleep in your embrace."

He peers into her irises. His pupils speak, understanding.

Rayne links their pinkies and leads Chase past the face down and forgotten teddy. They cocoon in the sink of her mattress. As their eyes shut, Chase's phone rings…and rings…until it rings no more:

JENAE

(1) Missed Call

13 Pebbles and Bam...Bam...Bam

❧

BUH DUMP BUMP BUMP

"Whoa, sorry 'bout dat suh. I didn't see dat deah pah-hole. No suh I didn't. No suh, no suh," says the cherub faced driver with a southern drawl.

His rickety Jeep Cherokee rumbles down the final stretch of Highway 301.

"It's fine," Chase mumbles. He squints in the backseat from the hazy Georgia sun. The last bit of cool was in the arrivals terminal at Savannah airport.

"Sorry 'bout the air conditionin'. Damn thing went out just before dispatch sent me to git ya'".

Chase doesn't respond. It's only the *third* time the chatty cab driver has mentioned this fact.

"Now dat deah is the Jesup waffle house. Best pork chops 'n eggs in the south yes suh, yes suh. And look over yonder. Out yo' left winduh. Bet y'all ain't got no two dollar drive-ins up north now do ya'? Yes suh, yes suh."

Chase is uninterested in the unremarkable scenery. He'd prefer the quiet. The motor mouth driver—in the nipple revealing mesh shirt—seems allergic to silence.

"So what was y'all winter like?" He does't pause for a response. "Ooh Lawd we had us a rough one. Not like y'all yankees but we had us some snow. A whole two inches. Believe that? Schools closed for damn near a week."

The chatterbox continues in a stream of consciousness. He is a blend of southern hospitality and the drunk uncle at the barbecue. To

Chase he's a bobblehead on a dashboard. A curiosity that gets old after the first couple of bobbles.

After twenty more minutes of car talk the vehicle slows and turns right at a flag pole. They drive down a hot asphalt driveway. The smell of fresh cut Kentucky bluegrass and compost seep into the vehicle. They stop in front of a one story brick building.

F.C.I. JESUP

Federal Correctional Institution

Jesup, GA

"I hope you ain't here to check in. Hahaha…whooo. That was a funny," the driver laughs with jiggling jowls.

"Can't park here. The visitor's lot is that way," Chase says.

The cabbie circles the jeep into an open parking space by a set of chainlink fences with barbed wire. A guard tower and grey barracks are in the distance. Chase exits the vehicle. He adjusts his black NYC logo baseball cap.

"Wait here. I should be no more than an hour," Chase says.

"Yup, yes suh I'm a man of my word. Extra twenty bucks like we agreed and Willy Ray Sykes will sit right cheah an' wait for ya', yes suh, yes suh. I don't know how dey do up north, but 'rounds here a man's word is his bond. That's right. You know that reminds me of this odd gentleman I waited a whole day fo' up near Savannah years ago. He was from Phil-delph…wait no, he was from Chicah—uh… no,no. I forget. Somewhere. Strange little feller. Wore a long coat and one of dem detective movie hats. A fuhnora, flora, sora—"

"It's called a fedora. You waited for a man in a fedora, sheesh," Chase says.

The driver purses his lips and cocks his brow at Chase.

Chase crunches the gravel path from the visitor's lot to the main building. When he awakened in Rayne's bed that next morning, her naked lungs inhaling with his own, he knew what had to be done. Eugene's threats have held him in suspended animation for over six months. But the costs are rising. The price is too much to bear. Chase has decided to defy explicit instructions not to contact the man on the recording. The recording that Eugene played for him in the dark, damp corridor at The Anatolia restaurant. He must appeal to the only person who can cut the thread unraveling the fabric of his life. And that man is a prisoner by the name of Angelo *Bam* Hickson.

Chase walks through the automatic doors and into an immaculate reception area. A single uniformed officer mans the chest-high circular desk. His gaze transfixed on a computer screen.

"Hi, I'm here to see—"

"I.D.," the officer says, without the courtesy of eye contact.

Chase pulls out his driver's license and places it on the counter.

"New York? Who are you here for?"

"Hickson. Angelo Hickson," Chase says.

"Bam? Hmm. He doesn't get many visitors. You have to be on the list."

The officer taps a few keystrokes. He looks at the screen and holds the I.D. to Chase's face.

"Okay, you're on his visitor list. Wrist."

Chase extends his arm.

"No, the other side. Like you're going to a club," he says. He stamps the back of Chase's palm with a UV light hand stamp. Chase signs the log.

"Proceed to security," he says.

The officer points Chase to the line at the metal detector. It's being held up by a woman in a neon yellow tube top that barely covers her surgically enhanced cleaving. She is arguing with the intake officer about the *appropriateness* of her clothing. Eventually they get to Chase.

"No hats," the burly corrections officer says.

Chase leaves his hat at security and enters the visitation area. Several tables are surrounded by loved ones and lawyers. All have men in khaki jumpsuits with numbers for names. But Chase doesn't see the one he is looking for. A guard taps his shoulder. He points him to a room divider where another guard stands as a sentry.

"You waiting for some special invite or are you gonna get your ass back here?"

The voice is a booming baritone. The guard lets Chase through. As he rounds the corner, his eyes are met by the chiseled jaw, shaved yellow cranium, and salt 'n pepper scruff of Angelo *Bam* Hickson.

"Well, look at you. Broad, rugged shoulders. Cock diesel arms. You look good ha ha," Bam says. His voice is a cocktail of Vincent Price and Dwayne *The Rock* Johnson. His laugh is James Earl Jones.

"How long it's been? Seven, eight years?" Bam says.

"Nine this summer," Chase replies.

"Nine? Well, I'll be a goddamn. I must be getting old."

"It took me a while to find you," Chase says.

Bam appears perplexed before realizing.

"Oh, right, right. Man, I got transferred out of Macon about six months after you got paroled."

Bam leans back in his chair. It exposes his silverback width. Though not particularly tall, he has the heft of a retired running back. He appears larger than his five foot seven inch frame would suggest.

"But you didn't fly all the way down here to shoot the shit did you?" he says.

"No, I didn't. And I would have come sooner. Or reached out or uh—"

"You still can't spit stuff out? After all these years you still worry about what people think? Don't let the fear of a reaction dictate *your* actions. Do you remember my two favorite letters in the English language?"

Chase pauses to ponder, then half-chuckles a response.

"F and U."

"Exactly. *Eff-You*. Middle finger to the goddamn world," Bam says, slamming his fist on the table.

The guard standing outside the divider pops in. Bam fumes.

"Did I ask you to stick your pink pecker in here?" he says.

The young guard freezes with his mouth open.

"Well, did I?" Bam says.

"Sorry Bam, I thought you needed some assistance."

Bam glares. The guard returns to his post.

"Still running things I see," Chase says.

"I do okay. So why you here, boy? When I handed you that Chase Marlon Archibald driver's license, passport, social security card, credit card, bank account, college gig…I told you to restart your life and never look back. You showing up here? That's the very definition of looking back." Bam leans to the side and draws Chase near…"Hey, did your real name resurface or something?"

Chase hesitates for a moment before answering.

"Well, yes and no," Chase says.

"You know I don't like guessing games. Crap or get off the crapper."

"Bam, I know you said not to contact you. You were quite clear and angry."

"Clear? Yes. But angry? I wouldn't say I was *angry*. I told you to forget your name. No more Tevarus Huxley. Forget your old life. The alcoholic, passive-aggressive father. The bipolar, drug addicted mother. And most importantly, that thing with the little white girl that got you sent to prison in the first place. Chase, I gave you something people just don't get in this world. A new start. A clean slate."

"Bam, I know but when Eugene played that recording of you getting upset because I wasn't following the plan, I—"

Bam's freckled face wrinkles. "Recording? Plan? What are you talking about? Eugene? You're talking my *son* Eugene?"

"Yes, Eugene played the—"

"He contacted you?"

Chase contorts his face.

"Bam, Eugene's been in contact with me since last Summer."

"In contact? As in, *on-going* contact? Last summer?"

Bam's bombastic voice blares. He slams his forearm on the table. The crash is so loud it hushes the murmur of conversations on the other side of the divider. The boyish guard who Bam dismissed earlier peeks his head in. Bam meets his sheepish gaze with a lion's stare. The young man shrinks back to his post.

Bam's lips ripple. His fiery freckles dissolve into his redbone complexion. Chase stares at Bam's hairy knuckles as they ball into rusty mallets. His snout pulses as he strains to compose himself.

"Eugene *visited* you?" Bam growls.

"Yes, he said you sent him," Chase says.

"*I* sent him?"

"Bam, he played your voice. You went ballistic."

Bam lifts his eyes towards the duct work above.

"Hmmm. I bet this so-called *recording* was played a few months ago?"

"Yeah. But why is this a surprise to you? You didn't send Eugene? You didn't come up with this plan for me to be a donor?"

"What? A donor? Why would I care about you donating blood?"

"No, not that kind of donor…" Chase leans in. "A *sperm* donor."

"A sperm donor? What kind of dumb ass plan is that?"

"Shhh, geez come on Bam."

"So, what are you doing? Squirting in a cup?"

"A cup? No, no…" Chase leans in again. "The plan is—"

"Stop whispering goddammit. I run this muthafucka. Speak your mind."

Chase straightens up.

"Okay, the plan is for me to…not squirt in a cup but…well…not to sound crass but…*squirt* in *them*."

"*Them*? Who the fuck is them?"

"The women," Chase murmurs.

"Impregnate women? That's the plan?"

"You make it sound so basic, but uh, yeah…basically."

Bam's wheels start turning.

"Let me guess. This was my idea and I was going to kick your ass or blow up your spot if you didn't do it? I protected you when you was in the joint. Got you set up when you got out. So since I created Chase Archibald that means you owe me. And if you refused to be down with this scheme, I was going to expose your true identity. You're Tevarus Huxley, an ex-con from Savannah, Georgia. Tevarus who never got a college degree, never lived in Boston, whose parents are still alive and the worst part he was convicted of the worst crime you can be convicted of. That about sum up his little plot?"

Chase lowers his head.

"Yes."

"Okay, I need details. The specifics. Start from the beginning. What was the plan? Who was involved? And how in the world do you make any money from it? I know that boy wouldn't do this without a big money pay off."

"Okay. It all started last summer. I was in a park when I got this cryptic note…" Chase gives Bam a detailed account of the plot. At certain points in the story, such as when Eugene crashed Chase's birthday party or when he played the audio at the restaurant, Bam erupts. He stomps around or pounds the table. When Chase mentions Andrea's involvement he screws his face.

"Hmm, something's not right about that one. You might want to keep your eye on that Andrea," Bam says.

After forty minutes of discussion Chase ends with...

"And then the driver dropped me off here."

"Mmmhmm," Bam nods. He folds his hairy *Popeye* arms across his chest and scans Chase's face like a finger running the page of a memoir. Chase's memoir. It is as if he can go back to the day an eighteen year old was escorted into maximum security at Macon State Prison. Chase was a flower of fear—an enticing aroma to the sadistic felons he was tossed in with. But it was Bam that protected the young Chase. And Bam asked for nothing in return.

"Well, someone's been a busy beaver," Bam says.

"Yes, I guess I have these past few months," Chase says.

"I am referring to Eugene."

"But Bam I don't understand. If you didn't even *know* about this, how did he record you getting mad at me?"

"He didn't. You fell for the okie doke. He didn't record me getting mad at *you*. He recorded me getting mad at *him*."

"I don't understand," Chase says.

"You were like a son to me. I would never act that way towards you. But you weren't the first young blood I helped. There was a guy before you. He wasn't someone that I created an entire new identity for like I did with you, but I helped him out. I got him a place in the city—New York—and a sweet gig as a stock broker. Smart guy, he just wouldn't have been able to land that job with a criminal record. So I what I do and got him hooked up. But against my better judgment, I used Eugene as my go between. One day, Eugene went behind my back and pressured they guy to get involved in insider trading."

Chase puzzles a thought.

"Wait…you said a stock broker?"

"Yes, why?"

Realization washes over Chase's face.

"*That's* why that dude left my party when Eugene showed up. I met your guy a couple of years ago when I was with Andrea. She does real estate on the side and got him a new apartment. They became more than friends after she and I broke up. Jenae and I met them for drinks once. We took a group selfie. Eugene made a smart remark to me about being careful who I took pictures with. That's the pic he must have been referring to. Eugene must have seen that pic when he was blackmailing your guy and he recognized me. Maybe in his office or something. Eugene always hated me. That connection is all Eugene needed to start digging for info on me. I never put it all together. But how does that factor into the recording?"

"If the broker got caught doing insider trading that would have landed him right back in prison. Then an investigation into how he never got flagged in the first place. That would lead back to me. I can't have blown covers leading back to me. And that's Eugene's fault. So I sent for him. We had a nice father/son chit-chat right where you're sitting. He brought his fat friend with him too. Must have been recording me…sneaky bastard. But they had to have done some major audio editing, Chase. I never even mentioned your name. That recording *had* to sound a bit off. Nothing was off about it?"

"No. I mean…hmmm, there were some spits and sputters. Distortions. But I didn't think anything of it. Bam, so much was going on. I was petrified. I thought I disappointed you somehow. That I was ungrateful and you would—"

Bam bolts from his chair and grips the back of Chase's neck. He pins Chase to the chair and points a menacing finger.

"Look at me. I would *never* do anything to hurt you. I protected you because I saw greatness in you. I wasn't going to allow your young life to get sucked down a rotten sewer. You get me?"

Chase nods.

"Does anyone else know about Tevarus Huxley? Jenae, Andrea? Your best friend…what's his name? Hiraka?"

"Tanaka. None of them know. But Jenae *has* been acting moody. I think she feels something isn't right."

"Eh. Women always think they *know* shit when they don't know shit. But watch that intuition," Bam says.

"Oh wait. Maybe Man-Man's cousin knows. The last woman I told you about? Rayne Chimes? She said Man-Man tells her everything. But she didn't seem to care about my past. She got all therapeutic on me. Actually motivated me to come visit *you*."

"So you love this girl?"

"Rayne?"

"No. Your fiancée, Jenae."

"Of course, I love her. That's why I agreed to this crazy scheme in the first place. I didn't want to lose her."

"Possibly. Don't get me wrong…I believe you love Jenae. But you also love this life I gave you. Maybe a little too much. That's why you were vulnerable to Eugene's demands. You were afraid of losing Chase and becoming Tevarus again."

"My name is Chase," Chase says.

"Of course it is." Bam smiles as if he's humoring a child.

The echoes of children visiting their incarcerated fathers billow around them.

"This Devantay. You've taken a shine to him?"

"Yes, he's a great kid. Intelligent. Clever, in fact. He's had a rough start. Drug addicted mom. Father committed suicide. Toxic relatives. All he has known is foster care and group homes."

"But you *see* something in him don't you?" Bam gets a gleam in his eye, and wags his finger at eye level waiting for Chase to agree.

"Yes. I do. He just needs love and guidance."

"Aha. You have that same eye that I do."

From behind the curtain a throat clears with a tepid, *ahem.*

"Buh-Buh-Bam. I'm sorry but visiting hours are over and dinner is going to start soon. I'm sorry but—"

"Relax, pecker wood. I know you still need to do at least a little bit of your job. We're done anyway."

The guard retreats.

"Done? But wait what about—?"

Bam rises and spreads his arms wide. They hug. Although Bam is much shorter, Chase feels smothered. He then stiff-arms Chase by the shoulders as if he's holding a baby with a dirty diaper.

"Listen here Chase. You won't have to worry about Eugene, or your career, or your engagement any longer. And no more of this banging chicks for tricks. Unless you're like most men who haven't matured and want sex without responsibility?"

"No. I just want my life back. *My* life," Chase says.

"I will take care of that. I will make sure you get your life back. Don't let pebbles down a mountain turn into boulders on your road. I'll fix it," Bam says.

Chase radiates a smile with a cyclone of relief. Bam's word is like the sunrise and the sunset. Guaranteed to happen.

"Go home, Chase," Bam says.

Bam calls for the guard. He escorts Chase back to security. Chase flashes the back of his palm under the UV light to re-enter the lobby. He grabs his cap and he steps into the blinding sun. There's a renewed pep in his step as he sashays to the jeep. The front is empty. The cabbie is in the back catching z's. Chase raps on the window.

"Huh, wha, oh sorry, sorry suh. I was just gittin' a bit of shut-eye. Didn't quite know how longs you'd be gone. Everything okay? Didn't get arrested did ya'? Uh hee hee heh. That was a funny."

"And a mighty fine one. Fine one indeed as *y'all* say."

"Well, well now. I sees we done made a mighty fine impression on ya'. Mighty fine. You about *ret tuh go* suh?"

"Quite ready," Chase says. The driver jumps behind the wheel.

"Hey, you mind if I ride shotgun?" Chase says.

The driver's white teeth shine bright.

"Mind? Why I don't mind at all. We can talk the whole way back to Savannah. The *whooole* way," he says, with a head bobble.

Chase hops in. As he settles in he feels something poke the seat of his pants. He reaches in the crease of the seat and pulls out a book.

"Oh, sorry about that suh. I do some reading in betweens fares."

Chase inspects the coffee ring stained cover but it isn't the condition of the book that strikes him. It is the very title itself:

Marmion: A Tale of Flodden Field
by Walter Scott, Esq.

The novel is noteworthy because it contains a well known quote that is often, though erroneously, attributed to William Shakespeare:

"Oh what a tangled web we weave,
When first we practice to deceive."

He tosses the book in the backseat. The driver cranks the ignition and shifts gears for Savannah Airport. It is the start of Spring. Three months before the fateful day that began our story.

14 Revelations 1

❧

Gotham. White smoke from molten tar stings his nostrils. He coughs but nothing breaks his stride. His gallop is spirited. He leaps and bounds with exuberance. Spring is rebirth. It's been a month since the trip to Jesup prison gave him a new lease on life. He hasn't had a surprise pop-up since. No veiled threats. No random women. And Jenae no longer withdraws from his caresses. All is right as rain. His legs circle the corner of Catherine Slip and down Water Street. He jogs past the halal street vendor on South Street. The savory aroma of lamb gyro and basmati rice has him considering a U-turn. That is until he hears a fragile voice ring his name.

"Buff Puff."

He turns only to see a line for the food cart and a blonde mother *push-jogging* a three wheeled baby buggy.

"Buff Puff," echoes again followed by sickly coughs.

Chase finally sees the source. It is Miss Pat. She is crouched on the pavement clutching her knees to her chest. Next to her is an orange construction cylinder. Her matted hair droops from her thinning scalp. She struggles to lift. Her follicles seem to weigh her down as if each end carries an anchor.

"Oh no, Miss Pat?" Chase says.

Her head wobbles. Chase kneels and palms her shoulder.

"Aww, Buff Puff. Look at you. Don't look so sad," she wheezes.

Chase takes out a half-filled aluminum canteen from his fanny pack. He cups her chin and trickles a bit of the water into her mouth. She scrunches her wrinkled face and spits up.

"Yuck. That's water," she cackles. Chase stares in disbelief.

"Of course it's water. What did you think I was giving you?"

"You ain't got no wine?" she says.

"No, Miss Pat. No alcohol."

"Bah," she says, and brushes the flask away.

"Miss Pat you need to drink something."

"It don't matter no way. My time's up," she says.

"What do you mean? Of course it matters."

"No, Buff Puff."

She curls into a violent fit of coughs.

"Miss Pat, let me help you up. We need to get you to a hospital."

She slaps his arms away.

"I told you my time is up."

"Miss Pat stop talking crazy."

The frail, spunky woman continues hacking. She crinkles a finger and beckons Chase to come closer.

"My time is d-d-done."

Her eyes flutter.

"Miss Pat, you're drifting."

Chase shakes her.

"Buff Puh—Chase. Chase we all got to go home."

"Miss Pat I am home. I live here."

"You don't live here, boy," she shouts.

She teeters like a buoy on an ocean wave. Chase steadies her.

"Okay, Miss Pat. Where do you think my home is?"

"Death. Death is your home. You need to die, Chase. You can't live until you die."

Miss Pat launches into a tantrum of coughs and gurgles. She collapses on her side. She shivers and chokes on her tongue.

"Miss Pat. Miss Pat. Somebody help. Hello, somebody help. Call 911. I said somebo—."

Chase rises. The street is suddenly empty. Silent. The food cart has vanished. There are no vehicles, no pedestrians. Not a soul. Just an eerie stillness. He kneels to lift Miss Pat but all of a sudden...she's gone! Chase is confused. He hyperventilates. He darts his eyes from corner to corner. He echoes her name. The sky turns grey. The sun goes dark. The street blurs. Everything goes to black.

And then a bright light spills into crevices of his eyelids.

He tosses from side-to-side and mumbles a delirious *Miss Pat, Miss Pat.*

"Babe," Jenae says.

"Miss Pah-Pah."

"Babe...Babe...wake up."

She shakes his shoulders. It snaps him out of his stupor.

"Hey baby. It's okay. It's me. You're here with me," she says.

She dabs a wet cloth on his brow.

"Wuh..was I talking in my sleep?" Chase says.

"You screamed, Miss Pat. Wasn't that the bag lady who kept popping up in your dreams last year?"

A groggy Chase sits up.

"Yeah. I don't remember much now, though. I just remember...babe? Babe, I think she died in my dream."

"Died? Maybe now you'll start jogging in *real* life. Ya' think?"

"Oh here we go," Chase says.

"Look, I love my man and his muscles. But you're getting older now. Think heart health. You need to do more than lift weights. The only time you ever did cardio was when you were running across the Brooklyn Bridge in a damn dream? Visiting homeless women."

"Woman. Singular. And babe, I don't control my dreams."

"I know, I know. But a dream can be a sign. As in maybe you should take up jogging for real? It is a beautiful bridge you know."

"Wait. You know what? I do remember something. So weird. She said I needed to die to live. Something like that."

"That's the subconscious talking. You keeping secrets from me?"

"Oh are you talking slick young lady? Huh? Huh?"

Chase rolls on top of Jenae. His bare chest compresses her camisole clad bosom. He rumbles his fingers up her sides. She bursts into an uncontrolled laughter.

"Chase…Chase…stop…ha…ha….stop," she laughs. "Oooh boy you're gonna guh-guh get ha ha ha."

She pops and jerks from his fiddling fingers. "Stop, okay, okay. You win…Whew…You win, you win baby ayeee."

Chase finally stops tickling. He collapses at her side. Both of them are out-of-breath. The huff and puff for several seconds.

"Babe, I want to tell you something," he says.

"Tell me later, handsome man." She rolls on top of him. "Let's work on that cardio."

Jenae peppers him with kisses.

"Mmm-Mmm-Babe-Wait-Babe," he says.

She freezes his head in her palms.

"Honey. You are *so* killing my vibe right now."

"Babe, I know, I know. But I just need to say this to you."

"*Now*, he wants to be sensitive. You see the mood I'm in, right?"

"Yes. And I promise to address every nook and cranny of your gorgeousness with copious amounts of attention—in a minute."

"G'head, g'ghead," she says, with a two-finger flip.

"So we had our rough patch a few months ago right?"

"Yeah. But you got it together after you came back from your conference in Boston. We're good," she says.

Chase bites his bottom lip as this reminds him of the lie he told Jenae to cover for his trip to see Bam in Georgia.

"I just want your mind at ease. I got it together. Everything has been better between us right?"

"Yes, Chase. I said we're good. Now babe, I really appreciate this warm and fuzzy, *I really need to share* moment of yours. Really I do. But we're good. Now, about those copious amounts of attention."

She peels his boxers back and laps her tongue into his. They kiss passionately for all of about two seconds. Chase pops his lips off.

"But you know I love you right? I mean, I seriously worked on some stuff. I was wrong. I was being evasive and impatient and acting like—"

"Good Lord, boy!" Jenae rolls her eyes back and flops her head onto the pillow.

"Babe I know, I know. I just wanted you to underst—"

The doorbell rings.

"You've got to be kidding me," Jenae says. "Are you expecting someone? Devantay? I know it better not be that big mouth Tanaka."

"I'm not expecting anyone today," he says.

Chase tosses on a tee and a pair of cotton lounge pants from the dresser. He pauses in the mirror. Jenae is pouting. He blows a kiss.

"Just hold that thought babe."

"Hmph," she grunts.

Chase scampers downstairs. As he walks to the door he sees the outline of two familiar figures through the double window pane. His suspicions are confirmed when he opens the door.

"Well, well, well. If it isn't Eugene Merriweather and Boy-Boy,"

"Chase," Eugene says.

"Chase? Oh, that's my name now? I'm not *playboy* anymore?"

"Look, I'm just here to apologize okay?" Eugene says.

Chase cups his hand to his ear.

"I'm sorry. To do what, now? Didn't quite catch that."

"I apologize," Eugene grits.

"That didn't sound too convincing. Hey, Boy-Boy. Help him out. What he say?…Come on chop, chop, I'm waiting?"

"He apologizes," Man-Man says.

Chase rifles his gaze from one to the other with the smuggest of grins.

"Let's not drag this out. We flew back and spoke to Bam. I was ordered to apologize so I did. You won't be seeing us again. Happy?"

"No, no, no. You don't get off that easily. You nearly destroyed my life, you bratty little shit. And why? Money? Envy? You've always had it out for me."

Eugene taps Man-Man's shoulder. They both start to leave.

"Whoa. Don't you walk away from me," Chase says. "Unless you want me to inform Bam?"

"Fine, say what you gotta say Chase," Eugene says.

"Look at what you did, Eugene. And for what? Because you have daddy issues? I didn't ask Bam to look out for me when we were all in prison. Treating me like his son. It's not my fault daddy never gave you a hug."

"I don't need this. I gave you your damn apolo—"

Chase snatches Eugene by the collar and twists. Man-Man makes a move towards Chase.

"Go ahead and try something, tubby. Go ahead."

Man-Man retreats. Eugene struggles as he chokes.

"You listen to me. You and your boy are going to *really* disappear…as in forever. Don't pass go, don't collect two hundred dollars. Never come near *me*, my *job*, my *woman* ever. If you do—"

"I-I know, I know-*ach-cuh-cucah*-Ch-Chase I'm ch-choking."

"Good. Don't ever come back. As in never. Never. Never. And that's *your* word for the day."

The seconds tick but Chase refuses to release Eugene. Eugene's eyes tear. The whites turn ruddy. Nosy, old lady Mahone from across the street, cowers behind her drapes. She keeps her *good* eye on the action. Chase finally releases his clutch. Eugene drops to his knees. He hacks, wheezes and spits up phelgm. Chase turns to Man-Man.

"Well, what are you waiting for? Scoop your shit and scram."

Chase savors an arrogant joy. Eugene staggers with Man-Man to an idling BMW X5. They hop in the SUV. It zips down Henry Street and disappears into the place of *never return.*

Chase double-steps the stoop, runs in the living room and yells up the staircase as he jogs up.

"Hey babe?…ready for some cardio?"

3 Months Later...

The day our story began

"Coco, Piña, Cherry…Coco, Piña, Cherry," sings the stout little woman in El Salvadoran neck beads. She cheeses a cheeky, rustic smile as Chase bustles past her Italian ice cart. Commuters and students also emerge from the subway tunnel below. They fan out in multiple directions from the corner hub locals call, the Junction.

Chase shuffles past the Midwood-Brooklyn businesses to the black stone steps of Tilden Hall. He jostles through the throngs of undergrads exiting their final classes to reach his office. He inserts a key into the brass keyhole and turns. There's an odd click.

CLUH-CLUH

He tries again with the same result. It won't turn. He inspects the key but finds no fault in it. He scans the hallway. As fortune would have it, the chief custodian is just down the hall. Chase waves.

"Mr. Jenkins. Hey, Mr. Jenkins over here."

A gaunt, stubble-cheeked man in army coveralls and paint splattered construction boots is crouching by a water fountain. He holds a monkey wrench in one hand. A pile of screws is strewn at his bent knee. He waves the wrench in response.

"Hey there, Professor Archibald," Mr. Jenkins says.

"Mr. Jenkins, can I get your assistance for a moment please?"

The custodian rises. He is slender with a slight hump. He has worked for Brooklyn University for 43 years. He spends most of days plugging, spackling, and spit shining the landmark building into 21st century shape. His haggard face is offset by an infectious smile and a grey handlebar mustache—dyed shoeshine black. He moseys down.

"Good morning Professor Archibald…more like afternoon now I s'pose. How are you this fine day?"

"Now, I've always said just call me Chase, Mr. Jenkins."

"Oh I know, I know. But it always brings me a small sense of pride to call you professor. You're too young to remember when nobody looked like you around here."

"I appreciate that. Listen, Mr. Jenkins the strangest thing…my key doesn't work."

"Hmm. Now that sure is a strange thing. Strange thing indeed, professor. Might I have a look?"

Chase hands him the keys. The jack-of-all-trades removes a pair of copper rimmed glasses from his breast pocket and places them on the tip of his nose. He examines the key in microscopic detail.

"Uh huh," Mr. Jenkins grunts.

"What?" Chase replies.

"Uh huh," (holding it up to the light)

"What Mr. Jenkins, what?"

"Well, of course it don't work," he says.

"What do you mean, *of course*?"

"This here is your old key. Why ain't you using the new one?"

"Old? New? What are you talking about?"

"Professor, your lock was changed this morning. Didn't they give you the new key?"

"Changed? Why? And by whom?"

"Dean Ganges had me call the locksmith around...oh lemme see..." He flips the face cover on the heirloom watch that's attached to a chain on his belt. "Eruh uh-uh...9:30 this morning. Right after your department meeting."

"Department meeting? What department meeting? Our meetings are always on Mondays."

"Well I don't know about Mondays, todays or tomorruhs. But ya' had a meeting. Must've been important. Don't usually see President Laczko 'round here."

"President Laczko was here? I'm the incoming chair of the department. How could there be a mee—? Never mind. I'll straighten this out. Thank you Mr. Jenkins. Is Dean Ganges still in her office?"

"I don't quite know. There was a whole bunch of folks in there. White boys in suits and briefcases and everything."

"Okay thanks," Chase says.

Dr. Ganges' office is up two flights of steps. Chase runs upstairs and down the corridor to the oak and glass door stamped with the words Department Chair. He knocks. Hearing no response he pokes his head in. There's Carol, the Dean's middle aged secretary, hunched over her desk and texting. Chase clears his throat to get her attention.

"Oh," she says. She pops and a jiggles as if she got the chills. "Excuse me Doctor Archibald, I mean Professor Archibald I mean, I— so—so um, yeah, uh, hey, how the hell are ya'? How's it hanging?"

Carol has always been a bit of an oddball. She wears pink feather boas, has a 400 song playlist—Prince albums only. She rarely completes a thought before starting another. And she talks with a lisp.

"Are you okay?" he asks.

She cups her smartphone and hides the screen on her lap. Chase finds her behavior peculiar...even for her.

"Mmmhmm, yup, yup, I'm fine. Why wouldn't I be fine? Everything's fine. Aren't you fine? I mean you are *foine* as in attractive fine but uh yeah I'm good."She flashes an exaggerated, toothy grin.

Chase peers down the hall behind her desk. The Dean's door is closed with the privacy curtain drawn. Chase hears muffled voices.

"Is she with someone?"

Carol bobs her jaw open and closed and raises her index finger as if about to speak. She says nothing—like a stuttering mime.

"Carol!" Chase says.

"Yes...see...she...ummm...so, what had happened was...."

"Just ring her please."

Carol hesitates.

"Carol," he barks.

She presses the speaker button on the desk phone and dials *71. After two rings Dean Ganges answers.

"Yes, Carol."

"Uh, Dean Ganges...um...Mister, I mean Doctor, I mean—"

Chase crouches into the speaker.

"Good Afternoon Dean Ganges it's Chase. Sorry to bother you but do you have a second?"

The line goes silent. He looks at Carol. She shrugs. As Chase is about to repeat the question he hears hushed tones and then...

"Okay, send him."

Chase paces to the Dean's door. He taps the window twice.

"Enter," she says.

Chase walks in. The office is spacious. Earth toned walls decorated with Masai and Sudanese art. The handmade six tier bookshelf is stocked with the classic and the contemporary. To Chase's right is a table and chairs stacked with moving boxes. Two are unsealed. Chase recognizes a framed picture of Devantay and himself, from a Long Island fishing trip, poking from one of the boxes. Perplexed, he stares at Dr. Ganges. She is sitting behind her beechwood desk with her arms folded. Her degrees from Spelman, Columbia and Rutgers hang proudly on the wall behind her. She has a visitor. To her left is a well tailored silver fox. A middle aged man in a pinstriped suit. He sports a full head of shiny, salt and pepper hair with slick comb marks. He half-sits on the edge of her desk, forearm on thigh, showcasing the big face Rolex wristwatch.

"Good Afternoon," Chase says. Dr. Ganges doesn't respond.

The man slides off the desk and extends a hand.

"Good afternoon, Chase. My name is Frank LaRocca. I'm an attorney with the university. You can call me Frank," he says.

"Attorney? Dean Ganges what's going on?"

"Why don't you have a seat, Chase," Frank says.

"I don't need a seat. And no offense Mr. uh…LaRocca is it? But I'm here to speak privately with my Dean."

"Anything you have to say, you say it in front of him," Dean Ganges says.

Chase is taken aback by her tone. He pauses then continues.

"Look, I don't know what's going on but my office is locked, there was a staff meeting I knew nothing about, I come here and Carol's acting nuttier than usual and now my desk has been cleaned out? Is this some sort of new leadership hazing ritual?"

"Hah, that's a laugh," Dean Ganges says.

"Look—" Chase attempts to say.

"No *you* look," she says, jumping up.

"Okay listen folks, let's keep our cool. We're all smart, educated people that can—," Frank says.

"*Some* of us are educated. *Some*," Dean Ganges says.

"Chase. Some news has been brought to the university's attention. It's serious. It's regarding your background," Frank says.

"It's about you being a goddamn fraud, Chase. Or whatever the hell your name is," Dean Ganges says.

Chase's heart thuds to the floor like a jilted lover.

"Oooh child," the eavesdropping Carol blurts from her desk. Frank shuts the door.

"Chase, Dean Ganges received that envelope right there," Frank says. He points to an open manila pouch. "Inside are some documents, photos and a letter. I'll read what it says."

"You don't have to read anything," Dean Ganges interrupts. "I'll tell you what it says. It says what you already know. Your real name is Tevarus Augustus Huxley," she says.

She slams her fist on the desk.

She might as well have fired two barrels from a sawed off. Chase feels like clutching his sternum. *This can't be right. Eugene left three months ago. He apologized. He said he'd never be back. Bam said he would take care of everything.*

"Oh you have nothing to say now?" Dean Ganges says. "You see he's not denying it, right Frank? You see that right?"

"Let's just talk about this," Chase says.

"Talk? About what? How you made a complete ass out of me? This department? This institution? For seven years? You wanna talk? Okay, let's talk about—let me see that Frank."

She snaps her fingers. Frank hands her the letter.

"Let's talk about…where is it?…Aaah. Here it is. And I quote: In this envelope you will find copies of a birth certificate, social security card, and high school photos of Tevarus Huxley who was born to Bernard Huxley and Terry Anne Mason who currently reside in Savannah, Georgia." The Dean ice-grills Chase. "You said your parents died in a car accident. It's a miracle. Jesus done resurrected mama and daddy."

"Dean Ganges I can explain," Chase says.

BUZZ...BUZZ

Chase's back pocket vibrates. He ignores it.

"Look at this. Fake transcripts, fake awards, phony letters of recommendation. It's all in the envelope. Mr. LaRocca called. Boston University where you got your alleged Bachelors? No record. The Attucks Academy for prep school? Never heard of a *Chase Archibald*. They did love the name though. You get a gold star for creativity."

"Dean Ganges if you would just let me explain. I can—"

"But wait...there's more. I haven't gotten to the best part."

Dean Ganges shoves a trembling fist of papers in Chase's face.

"Here. Read it. First page. Now."

Chase swallows and takes the packet. He reads the top page. His eyes bulge, his heart skips. *Oh no. No, no, not that.* It's Chase's felony record. Chase reaches for her. Dean Ganges shivers away.

"N-now look Dean Ganges. I can explain. It's what it seems."

Dean Ganges refuses to lay eyes on Chase.

"Octavia please," he says.

Upon hearing Chase speak her name aloud she cries out.

"CHILD MOLESTER! CHILD MOLESTER! You're a convicted child rapist."

"O-O-Octavia—"

"Frank and I searched the Georgia sex offender list online. Just to make sure.Your name is there. Your *real* name. Tevarus Augustus Huxley. You're a child molester."

Her words claw into his chest and rake his heart. He's been sucker punched. While a phony resumé is bad. And a criminal record worse. The violation of a child? That is the darkest truth that will destroy even the brightest lie.

"You betrayed me. You hurt me," she says as tears trickle. "You were more than a member of my staff. More than my closest colleague. You were like...you were like my own..."

"Your own son," Chase mumbles, head lowered.

"And the girl you did that to...my God...you disgust me."

"I didn't molest—"

"You didn't penetrate a minor child as your conviction states?"

"No. I mean sort of. Yes, but—"

"Get out," she says.

"Octavia let me—"

"Get Out. Get out. Get out."

She hurls papers and pounds the desk. Dean Ganges has never reacted like this. Emotion pours from both of them. Her disillusion devastates him. She lowers her head and points to the door.

"Chase just leave. Just...go."

Frank puts an arm around Dean Ganges. She shrugs him off.

"Come on Chase. We both should leave."

Frank turns the knob and opens the door. A crouching Carol tumbles inside. They ignore her and side-step. Frank escorts Chase into the silence of the second floor corridor.

"Look at you. You're a mess. Come on. You need to splash some water on your face," Frank says.

They enter the men's room. A lone, stumpy man is in the mirror. He's combing over the three remaining strands of his balding head.

Frank snaps his fingers in Bensonhurst fashion.

"Hey you. Yeah, you buddy. Scram, baldylocks."

"Have you no manners sir? I'm not going anywh—hey what the hell are you doing?" the man says.

Frank roughhouses him by the collar and tosses him out. The ruffled academic storms down the corridor vowing to fetch security.

Chase finds the strong-arm tactic surprising for a corporate lawyer but is too preoccupied with his own emotions. He sobs over the sink.

"Here, pull yourself together," Franks says.

He hands Chase a damp paper towel.

"Here's the deal Chase. Unless you prefer Tevarus?"

"It doesn't matter. It just really…doesn't matter."

"I'm not going to sugarcoat anything. You're in a pickle."

"Thank you Captain Obvious."

"Hey. Weisenheimer. Sarcasm ain't your friend right now. Pay attention."

"Just say what you have to say, man."

Chase's phone vibrates again. He slips his hand in his pocket and silences it. He gestures in the mirror for Frank to continue.

"Okay, so we've kept the circle of knowledge on this thing tight. So far only the president, head of the board, and vice-chancellor are aware of this situation. Oh and of course Dean Ganges. I can muzzle that goofy Carol lady with a few greenbacks. So that means this can be handled on the hush hush mush mush."

"Look, Mr. LaRocca. I'm not a child molester."

"Chase. You did five years at Georgia State Prison in Macon."

"I'm not disputing the fact that I did time but if I could just explain to Dean Ganges and President Laczko we can work this out."

"How are you going to *work out*, child molestation?"

"Stop saying that. I didn't—"

"Okay, okay don't yell at the friendly barrister here. Honestly? That's not even the biggest issue. Regardless of the charge, you're still a freakin' fraud. Your name is Huxley *not* Archibald. You grew up in Georgia, not Boston. Your parents are alive, they ain't dead. You never even graduated high school. How can you keep a job as a professor?"

Chase digs his fingers into his scalp and cries at the ceiling.

BUZZ BUZZ

He presses the ignore button again.

"Look, I'll share something with you, off the record okay?"

Chase closes his eyes and nods.

"This thing is a public relations nightmare. To have a child mole —excuse me—*person* with your background, teaching students barely out of their teens? Christ almighty, let me tell you. Heads would roll down Nostrand Avenue all the way to the Belt Parkway. Millions of dollars in lawsuits. And God forbid some hot blonde coed from one of your writing classes accused you of something."

"That's not who I am? I can't believe this is happening to me."

"All I'm saying is that the university wants to keep this quiet. But we have something else to discuss."

BUZZ BUZZ

"Look your phone's been buzzing like crazy. Just answer it. Then go home. Go *straight* home. I'll be in touch this afternoon."

Frank exits. Chase removes the vibrating phone from his pocket. His brow twists as he doesn't recognize the 718 number.

"Hello?" he says. "Wait. What? Who?...I'm sorry who is this?... Slow down...I can't understand...Devantay? Hey little man calm down, calm down. What's the problem?... What do you mean you overheard something about me? Wait, you're breaking up."

Chase squints as he struggles to hear. He puts a finger in his other ear and walks out of the bathroom for better reception. He finds a secluded corner near the end of the hall and cradles the phone to his mouth.

"Okay, go ahead Devantay," Chase says.

"Cake overheard the director Mr. James on the phone. He said he kept hearing something about how you got a fake name and was in jail for something real bad. Then Cake cracked the door open a little, and he saw some papers and pictures of you in Mr. James' hand. Mr. James was really upset."

Chase drops the phone. Another sonic boom to his torso.

"Chase? Chase? Hello? Chase?" the receiver squeaks from the floor. Chase gathers himself and picks it up.

"I'm still here Devantay. I'm here."

Chase bolts down the stairwell with the phone to his ear.

"Chase, I don't understand. Cake said Mr. James was yelling about how your name is *Various* or *August* or something, I don't know. That you went to jail because you touched a little girl and—"

"What else?" Chase says.

Chase power-walks past his locked office and out in the sun onto the congested Flatbush Avenue pavement.

"Cake said you escaped from jail and—"

"Escaped? Listen to me Devantay. There's some grownup stuff going on right now that I can't explain."

"Chase I don't understand. Did I do something wrong?"

"Little man no, no. Don't ever think that. You didn't do anything. Someone is trying to ruin everything I've built. It's not your fault. I'm going to figure this out. You just—hello? Hello, Devantay? Devantay what's all that I hear in the background?"

Chase can hear Devantay's voice being shouted over. There's a shuffling sound. An older man's voice jumps on the call.

"Give me that phone Devantay," the voice says. "Hello? Is this the so-called Chase Archibald?"

"This is Chase. Where's Devantay? Who is this?"

"This is Amos James, Director of the Bedford-Stuyvesant Boys to Men Leadership Academy and Group Home. And you don't get to ask the questions."

"Come on, Mr. James. You know me. We've spoken several times."

"Look, Mr. Archibald...excuse me, I mean convicted felon Tevarus Huxley. I'm going to make this quick. You are to have no further contact with Devantay and you are to never, I repeat *never* to come near him or these premises."

"Noooo," Devantay yells in the background.

"Hey, put Devantay back on the phone," Chase says.

"You don't give the orders," Mr. James says. "I swear to you. If it weren't for the negative publicity it would bring to this institution, the grant money we would lose, the people who would get fired, I would turn your ass in right now. Stay away Huxley."

"No. Chase, Chase what's he saying?" Devantay wails.

"Stop, Devantay. Don't grab at the phone. Chase is a bad man and you're not seeing him anymore," Mr. James says.

Devantay continues to shout in the background.

"Chase. Come get me. I want to be with you."

"Listen, Mr. James. Let's just—"

"No *you* listen. There's no discussion. You're a goddamn pedophile and a jailbird and that is the *last* thing this child needs in his life. Hell, I'm going to have to have a conversation with him to see if you touched *him* you sick fu—"

"I am NOT a pedophile," Chase screams at the phone. His outburst causes pedestrians to freeze and gawk as if he were naked.

"I don't give a damn what your story is. Your relationship with Devantay is over. And you only have yourself to blame."

"Chase, what's happening?" Devantay says.

"Mr. James, please. Let me at least…let me at least say goodbye. Can you do that? Not even for me. Do it for him. At least let Devantay be able to say goodbye," Chase begs.

The prospect of losing Devantay forever is a dagger in his heart. Mr. James is silent. Devantay wails. After a moment Mr. James speaks.

"You have thirty seconds."

"Thirty seconds?"

"Or zero, take your pick."

"Okay, okay put him on."

Devantay comes back to the phone.

"Chase. Chase what's happening? What's he talking about?"

"Hey, hey now little man. I know I taught you better. I hear you crying. Chin up. Chest out. Wipe those tears okay?…I said *okay*?"

"Y-Y-Yes Chase," Devantay sniffles. "But I don't understand."

"I have to be quick. I did something in my past. Now it's not whatever nasty rumor you're hearing. And I didn't escape from anywhere. I served my time. But we're going to have to kind of…kind of have a timeout for a while. Just until I sort this out."

"Timeout? What do you mean? For how long? What did I do?"

"Nothing. This is on me. Just remember everything I taught you. Be good. Do good. Believe in yourself. Tell the truth. Okay?…Okay?… I can't hear you young man."

"O-okay."

"Let's wrap this up, Huxley," Mr. James says in the background.

"And remember. No matter what. I love you."

"And that hurts. Just like I said it would. Remember? Everybody who says I love you… hurts you."

"Devantay, no it's not like that. Listen it's—"

Chase hears the echo of crying footsteps running away.

"You had your thirty seconds."

"Look Mr. James let me—"

CLICK

"Hello? Hello? Mr. James? Mr.…."

Silence. The Brooklyn streets can't deafen Devantay's final words. Chase remembers the day Devantay uttered them. That was the day he told Devantay about his undying love for…love for…

Oh shit…Jenae!

15 Revelations 2

✧❧✧

"Jenae," Chase shouts, in the middle of the sidewalk.

Chase is realizing the full breadth of what is happening. His career is in shambles. The child that was a son has been abducted from his heart. What's left? Not *what...who?* He seldom calls Jenae at her office so he has to fire his thumb through his contacts for the number.

It rings...and rings...and rings...*Come on, come on, come on, pick up, pick up, pick—*

"Good Afternoon, Metzger and Weiss. How may I direct your call?"

"Hi...um...Gi-selle, Giselle right? It's Chase. Jenae's fiancée. We met at the holiday party, remember? Is she in?"

"Oh hello, Mr. Archibald. Ms. Dixon is gone for the day. She left a couple of hours ago."

"Gone for the day? Is she in court? She was supposed to be in the office all day?"

"She was but she got called into a meeting with the partners around eleven. An hour later she came out and said she was leaving for the day. Personal business. She looked flushed. I hope she's okay."

"Did she say where she was going?"

"I'm sorry, Mr. Archibald, no. But she did make a call before she left. It sounded like she was meeting someone at your place. I thought she was meeting up with you."

To keep appearances Chase says, "Oh. Yes. Silly me. Slipped my mind. I was supposed to meet her at my place. Thanks."

"No problem. Have a nice day."

Chase dials Jenae's mobile. It goes to voicemail.

"Ugh, come on," Chase says. He hangs up and dials again.

"Hi, you've reached Attorney Jenae Dixon. I'm sorry I'm not—"

"Argh, Argh, Argh."

Gotta get home, Chase says and hangs up.

He opens an app on his phone to summon a ride. The closest vehicle happens to be parked near the Italian ice cart. It takes only a minute to scoop him up from the corner.

It's an agonizing twenty minute ride through the borough back to his Cobble Hill neighborhood. The black Camry finally reaches Henry street. It crosses the intersection of Baltic when they are forced to crawl behind a snail paced garbage truck. It takes up the entire roadway and reeks of all that is spoiled and rotten. Chase fidgets in the backseat. Pedestrians are moving faster than his ride-for-hire.

"Forget this. I'll hop out here," Chase says to the driver. "My brownstone is just down the block anyway."

Chase sprints down his sapling lined street. As reaches his five step walkup he finds his front door propped open by his potted cactus. Across the street old lady Mahone, the Jamaican neighbor with a long nose for other people's business, pretends to sweep her already spotless bottom stoop. Chase waves a nervous hello. She turns up her nose and sucks her teeth Caribbean style—long and loud. Keys tingle from Chase's doorway. It's Jenae's sister, Shauntelle.

"Shauntelle? What are you doing here? Where's your sister?" he says.

Shauntelle freezes on the top step of the stoop and screws her eyebrows down at him. She hoists a hefty bag on her shoulder and elbows past him toward an idling minivan.

"Shauntelle. Shauntelle, I'm talking to you. Where's your sister?"

"I don't got shit to say to you and neither does Jenae."

Her chocolate arms dump the heavy plastic bag in the backseat. A pair of Jenae's jeans flop out. Chase's eyes pop. As he turns to bolt up the steps, a teary eyed Jenae appears in the doorway.

"Babe, babe what are you doing?" he says.

She ignores him and clanks an overstuffed suitcase out of the brownstone.

"Babe, stop. I asked you a question."

He grabs her arm. She glares back. Her hazel brown eyes are pink and puffy. She blinks with a sniffle and a trickle.

"Get your paws off of me," Jenae says.

"Babe, listen. I know you're upset. Let me ex—,"

"Negro, please," Shauntelle says. "Get out of my sister's way."

Jenae snatches her arm from Chase's grip. She rolls the suitcase to the curb. He fires a stiff finger at Shauntelle.

"Mind your damn business, Shauntelle. This between us."

Shauntelle looks him up and down. Then she gets up in his face.

"I always knew you was hiding something. Ain't *no* man *that* damn perfect."

Jenae stomps back toward the steps. Chase blocks her.

"Baby, please. What you heard isn't the whole truth."

"You're in my way," she says.

"Baby, at least let me try to—"

"Move," Jenae says.

Ms. Mahone bends her ear to the action. She continues to sweep her immaculate porch.

"Sweetheart, don't act this way. That's not how we do," he says.

Jenae shoots her arms to the sky.

"How *we* do? What *we* are you talking about? I don't know you anymore. I never did. You were nothing but a lie. You played me for a fool. I can't think. I can't breathe. I-I can't…I can't *anything*. I wasted four years of my life on your lying ass. Four years."

"Mmmhmm that's right sis, you tell him. He ain't shit [she turns to him]. You know you ain't shit right?"

"Bud out, Shauntelle...Now babe, please. I can explain."

"Don't touch me," she says.

"Sweetheart you don't understand. This whole day has been the day from hell for me."

"For *you*? Are you serious? You have no idea what you put me through do you? Do you? I gave you my heart, my soul, my body. I promised myself to you. I let you put this damn rock on my finger. And you were nothing but a fake."

"Fraudulent...Bitch. Ass. Liar," Shauntelle says. She screws her index finger into his temple. He *shoulder-shrugs* it from his face.

Jenae cuts in.

"I had to find out about you at my law firm? In front of all of the partners? My colleagues?"

"Babe, I-I-I'll make this right. I'll tell them you knew nothing about this. I don't want you to get fired for my mistake."

Shauntelle *CLAP CLAP CLAPS* in his face.

"Hey, dummy. It's bad either way. Either she knew about your shit—which makes her a trifling ass liar like you—or she *didn't* know about your shit—I repeat—*YOUR* muthafuckin' shit, which means she got played by a player. That would make her boo-boo the fool. You ever seen Attorney *boo-boo* on a business card? So since you wanna *explaaain* shit, explain that one *bruh?*"

Chase scans the treelined block. The commotion has brought several neighbors out of their homes. He leans into Jenae's ear and says, "Can we discuss this inside please?"

"Oh hell no. No, no, no," she says, with a finger wag. "You don't get to keep hiding. You destroyed my world. Why do you get to keep yours a secret?"

"You tell him sis," Shauntelle says.

Chase grits his teeth and side-eyes her.

"Don't look at me like you fittin' to do something. 'Cause ya' ain't."

"Listen, babe. I-I messed up. But this has all been a big—"

"A big what? Misunderstanding? Mistake? Oh wait. Let me guess. It's a conspiracy. Have you forgotten that I'm a lawyer? I've heard it all."

"Actually, it kind of is all of those things if you would just—"

"Oh my God. This punk bitch here," Shauntelle says. She tosses her hands in the air. "Sis, let's get the rest of your stuff and leave this clown on the street with the rest of the trash."

Shauntelle pushes him aside and scoots up the steps. Her brokenhearted sister hurries up the stoop behind her.

"Babe wait. Babe"—he drops to his knees—"Please. Baby I love you."

Jenae pauses at the top. She stiffens her arms. Clenches her fists. And pivots in slow motion.

"You *love* me? What do you know about love?…Answer me."

"Babe, I—"

"Love? Love is when a woman's heart opens from a man's smile. Love is when she ignores her eyes and believes his tongue."

"Lucifer," Shauntelle shouts.

"Love is having to tolerate catcalls all day but getting to come home to a man that respects you…cradles you…protects you at night. Love is knowing he'll always want to dance to the music in our heads, lock pinkies on a stroll through Central Park, grow old and grey on a porch, and act silly together for no damn reason at all. I thought you knew how to love. No. You only know how to hurt."

She hovers above as he remains on bent knees. Her eyes burn with the heat of boiled tears. Without hesitation Chase leaps to his feet. He seizes her shoulders and forces a kiss. She squirms and wriggles in his vise-like clutch. He sticks his tongue into her resistant mouth.

"Mmph. Argh. Ugh. Mmph," she protests. His lips refuse to release their lock.

Shauntelle comes bounding down the steps towards Jenae but before she could interrupt, he screams in pain and grabs his mouth.

"Ow. Argh. " He hunches over. A drop of blood drips from his split tongue.

"You bih me," he slobbers, not able to pronounce the t.

"That's right girl bite him. Bite his ass. Crunch that shit," Shauntelle says. "Oh you thought you was gonna shove your nasty, lying tongue down my sister's throat and she was just gonna melt in your mouth? Why? 'Cause you said, *I love you?* Well you done learned today didn't ya'? How your tongue feel now, mumble mouth?"

Salty rivers flow down his cheeks. His lips part for the only words he can muster…

"But I love you."

Those three words ignite Jenae's ire. She paces up and down the rough concrete. Arms flailing. Head pounding. Tears overflowing.

"I *hate* you. I hate you. I hate you. You humiliated me. You hurt me. You destroyed *us.* You ripped my heart out. I-I-I can't think. I-I can't talk. I can't breathe. I-I-…You know what? Forget it. Keep whatever is left in that house. Keep it all. I can't stand the sight of you. I can't stand the smell of you. I can't stand the taste of you."

HACH-TUCH-SPIT

She spits in his face. Shauntelle smirks with pride.

The thick glob slugs down his cheek. He doesn't wipe it off. Jenae trembles. Shauntelle rushes to her aid. She smoothes her palm over her sister's cries. And kisses her forehead.

"Shhhh. It's okay sis. You gonna be alright. I got you. Come on. Let's go home."

Shauntelle braces Jenae on her shoulder and ushers her into the minivan. She, herself hops in the driver's seat. They drive up the block but Shauntelle pauses at the vehicle at the corner. She shifts into reverse. Chase's heart smiles with hope as the van returns. He rushes towards the passenger door. The love of his life rolls down the window…leans out, and throws a perfect strike that clinks off his forehead. He looks at the pavement. The afternoon sun shimmies off the diamond engagement ring. It has just landed in a hot pile of dog shit. Shauntelle leans from the driver's seat to make eye contact with him. She sucks her teeth and gives him the finger. Jenae buries her face in her palms. The van *vrooms* up the street, turns the corner and she's gone. As the black exhaust from the tailpipe dissipates, a voice chirps from the curb.

"Wow. That is *literally* a poetic pile of shit."

Chase sniffles. He rubs his blurry eyes as the voice comes into focus with a face.

"LaRocca? The school attorney? What are doing at my house. You following me?" Chase says.

Frank leans over the mound of manure. Practically studying it.

"Following you? No. I've been sitting in that Audi over there watching the shit show…like I said…literally."

"Great, now I have a corporate stalker. Let me tell you something motherfu—"

"Whoa, whoa, relax there big guy. I'm not stalking you."

Frank raises his palms and steps back.

"Remember in the restroom I said you should go home? That was because I was expecting this call."

Frank displays his cell phone.

"A call?" Chase says.

"I wanted to prep you earlier for this call but things were a bit intense. So I figured I'd catch up with you here but your girlfriend and her sister had other plans huh?" he says with a light chuckle. Chase screw-faces. "Uh, right. Here. Just take the call."

"I'm not interested. I've had enough surprises today. I know the bastard that did this. And I'm going to figure out how to find him."

Chase steps towards his door. A voice shouts from the speaker phone in Frank's palm.

"Chase, get back here."

Chase halts. The voice is familiar.

"Bam? Wait that can't be—"

"Yeah, it's me boy. Take the damn phone."

Chase is confused as to how this is possible. Frank hands him the receiver. He puts the phone to his ear.

"I don't want to see your earwax," Bam says.

"Huh?" Chase replies.

"I'm on video."

Chase cups the phone in both palms.

"Bam, how are you on video? You got out that quick?"

"Does it look like I'm out?"

Bam pans the camera around. It is the same secluded grey area they met in three months ago.

"Why are you so surprised that I can be on video from prison? You know who I am. But we have matters to discuss, don't we?"

"Hell yes we have *matters*. Starting with that asshole son of yours. Bam, whatever Eugene told you about leaving me alone? He lied. He didn't go away like he promised. He just laid low. Until now. Today he sent letters—"

"Chase," Bam says.

"Sent letters to the school, Devantay's group home—"

"Chase."

"And the worst thing, Bam? The worst thing? This snake. This-this fucking weasel. He goes and sends one to Jenae's job. My fiancée's job Bam!"

"Chase, you're not listening."

"We gotta get this dude. Where is he? I need your help finding him. I want to know where he is right now."

"Chase stop pacing back and forth you're making me dizzy. Eugene is right here."

Chase stops.

"Here? What do you mean? He's visiting you right now?"

"Chase, where's Frank? Frank, Frank can you hear me?"

"Yeah Bam. I'm right here," Frank hollers from a maple tree he's been leaning against.

"Wait a sec that reminds me," Chase says. "How the hell do the two of you know each other? Bam, this guy is a lawyer. He was in Dean Ganges' office when she threw me out of the building."

"First of all calm down. What have I always tell you about business? Look around."

Chase dots his gaze from house to house and street corner to street corner. All eyes are on him.

"Never put my business out in the street."

"Exactly. Take this inside," Bam says.

Frank walk up the stoop go through the foyer and enter the living room. Chase chokes as the clear visual of Jenae's absence punches him in the gut. Paintings, sculptures and knick-knacks from their trips abroad have disappeared. But he has no time to sulk. Chase props the phone on the mantle. Bam's giant head and red freckled jowls fill the screen. Chase sits on the edge of the sofa.

"Better. Hmmm, nice place you got. Alright so listen up because I don't have much time. Eugene is here. As an inmate. I had Frank put me in touch with him. I made him turn himself in."

"Turn himself in?"

"Some old extortion stuff Frank kept a file on. We dropped dime on him and then Frank pulled some strings to get his extradition to Georgia expedited. I made him cop a plea to avoid a long trial and called in a favor with a judge to send him here. I need that boy near me. I realized that after what he tried to do to you. He won't be here forever. Just long enough for me to straighten him out like I should have. Frank hooked it up real nice. He's good with shit like that. He's the best Italian-Jew lawyer in the business. Ain't that right Frankie?"

"And you're the craziest biracial, mulatto, octaroon, ethnic mutt I've ever met," Frank says, poking his head into the field of view. The two men yuck it up.

"What the hell? You two are besties or something?" Chase says.

"Let's just say we go way back. I owe Bam my life," Frank says.

"Same here. A few times," Bam replies.

"Okay, whatever. Enough of this senior citizen buddy flick. Bam, I'll be on the next flight down there," Chase says.

"No, you won't," he replies.

"Bam, Eugene destroyed my life. Hell…he lied to *you*. You should be just as upset about this as I am."

"Chase."

"You know how you get when people are disloyal and disobey."

"Chase."

"He sent packages to everyone that matters to me. Why is this even a debate?"

"Chase, Eugene didn't send the packages I did."

"Eugene needs to pay for what he—wait—what? What did you just say?"

Chase's anger is replaced by total and complete confusion.

"You look shell-shocked. I get it. But yes, Chase. I was the one that sent the packages. With Frank's help."

"I don't under—how could?—-But why would?"

"Frank's firm has been under contract with the university for years. He has connections with the administration."

"I know where the bodies are buried so I can call in some favors," Frank quips.

"It's how we got you through the Masters program without you ever having done a Bachelors. How you got full tenure as a professor so quickly. Hell, it's one of Frank's dummy corporations that owns your brownstone. It's been nice only having had to pay utilities on a million dollar home hasn't it?"

"Gee, thanks," Chase says.

"Don't act like an ingrate. You're a convicted child molester."

Chase flinches.

"Kid, I know you got a raw deal. But I didn't meet you until you got inside. Your case was already settled. There were no strings I could pull. And your case was high profile in Georgia. The best I could do was set you up for a new identity when you got paroled. I set you up in Brooklyn because I'm a native. I still got peoples like Frank. He had the connections to give you a fresh start. A new life."

"If you did all that to create a new life for me why would you destroy it? You did exactly what Eugene threatened to do. You exposed me."

"It's simple Chase. You needed to die. I had to kill you."

Chase turns a perplexed stare at Frank. Frank shrugs.

"What the hell does that mean?" Chase says.

"Tevarus Huxley was a tall, athletic, gifted high school senior. Both on the football field and in the classroom. But when it came to street smarts? Kid, you were young and dumb. You walked down D block that day smelling like innocence and looking like candy."

"I *was* innocent. I'm not a—"

"I meant a different kind of innocent. The kind that's like perfume to these monsters in here. I seen young boys like you come in, get turned out, ripped apart, and I didn't think much of it. I got a heart but I ain't Superman. And I didn't get to be on top of this game by taking pity on every stray pup."

A guard comes into the frame and talks in Bam's ear: "Bam, we gotta cut this short. Warden's about to do a sweep."

"Alright I gotta make this quick. I saw something in you. You had a light, Chase. And I could see that you *really* shouldn't be in the joint. So I had my people look into your case. Didn't like how it went down for you. And then they sent you to a hell hole with murderers, sadistic Jeffrey Dahmer white boys and rapists that ain't finished raping. You reminded me of what I should have been to Eugene. Shit, I think the only time I ever hugged that little son-of-a-bitch was the day he was born. Anyway, you spend enough time locked up, all you have are your thoughts…and those thoughts start yelling your ugly truths. That you need to make shit right. You can't win if you ain't right within…a verse from a song I think…anyway you showed up right when I was having…a *moment*. I had issues with Eugene. You were my way of making up for not being who I should have been. So I took you under my wing."

"How does that translate into you blowing up my world, Bam?"

"If Eugene could find you and blackmail you that meant anyone could. *Tevarus Huxley* would always be circling like a vulture. And that's leverage. Leverage leaves you vulnerable. And someone could connect the dots back to Frank and me. I can't have that. Not even for you. So I took away the power of leverage. I neutralized that threat."

"That wasn't your decision to make. This is *my* life."

"But that's just it, Chase. It wasn't *your* life was it? It was *my* life. I created Chase Archibald. So, I killed Chase Archibald. So that Tevarus Huxley could live."

"That's fucked up Bam. You promised you would fix this," Chase says.

"I did fix it. One day you'll realize that."

"You didn't fix *anything*. You destroyed *everything*."

"Things unraveled because you weren't living your truth. You were living a lie."

Chase refuses to accept the possible truth in Bam's words.

"You're smart. Ambitious. I didn't create that. It's always been there. You'll be alright. But I've done all that I can do for you. It's time for you to live."

"Jenae?" Chase says.

"I can't fix a woman's heart. But I hope you can work it out. You're going to move out of the house, find yourself a job, and figure out your life. Frank got you legit Tevarus Huxley documents. Driver's license, passport, credit cards, all that. And I put five figures in your new bank account. Won't last forever in New York City but it gives you a start. It's time to fly on your own young blood. This is the last you'll see of me."

"What?"

"I don't believe in long ass goodbyes. Now give your girl some time to herself. When you do a woman wrong you need to honor the time she needs to sort her feelings. Maybe she'll come around. Maybe she won't. As for Devantay? I can't fix that one either. The home won't allow you back in his life. You're just going to have to own the damage this has done to him."

"The damage *you* have done. You messed up my life Bam. I had a good life."

"No. You had a good *lie*. There's a difference. Gotta go kid. Like I said. I don't do long goodbyes."

VIDEO CALL ENDED

THE DONOR

Chase sighs. The mid-afternoon sun casts a golden glow on his chiseled cheeks. Rivers of dry tears crust under his lashes. All is quiet. Silence can be a welcome comfort. Not even Frank speaks. Chase rises. He walks to the colossal bay windows and peers out. Frank reclines like a dignitary in a chair. He allows Chase this uninterrupted monologue with his own thoughts. After fifteen minutes, Chase breaks the calm.

"My favorite drink is ginger beer. Want one?" he says, without averting his pupils from the window.

"I've never had one. Why not? Thanks Chase," he says.

Chase slogs toward the kitchen as if he were towing sandbags with his ankles. He pauses and says…"Call me Tevarus."

16 Ashes, Ashes, We All Fall Down

👐

A singing preacher once said, *Love will make you do right, Love will make you do wrong.* It's been 2 ¹/₂ years since that day in May. Tears on his and her pillows have dried. A plethora of ignored phone calls, blocked texts, and a sister's insults have faded. And popping up at her office, pleading for forgiveness, only got him escorted out by security—twice. But time allows wounds to crust, scab and heal. And if you add some distance, even a scar will fade. So he moved to Jersey.

Montclair is a trendy enclave twenty-five minutes west of Manhattan. Some call it the Princeton of northern New Jersey—with a rustic smile. The only chain restaurant is a Starbucks nestled in a cul-de-sac. There's an indie bookstore that reeks of sweet pulp. You can delight in a salted caramel macaroon at the French bakery—run by a real Parisian. And a block from the art museum is the comforting and comfortable teashop with the clever name—*No EmpTeacup (we do free refills)*. Chase strolls through the door.

70's Soul streams from the ceiling. Red velvet love seats provide the decor. Chase creaks the floor boards as he strides past the ankle-high platform stage. He is greeted by AJ the barista. AJ wears a bull nose ring, lathers thick black mascara, and sports a faux Mohawk.

"Hey, how's it goin,' AJ?" Chase says.

"It's goin'. Looking forward to Halloween next week. Your usual?" AJ says. Chase nods.

"Grandé Pearl Jasmine Matcha Tea with soy, and an apricot jam biscuit," he shouts to his coworker at the bar.

Chase pays with an app on his phone. He sits at one of the wooden tables filling the center of the toasty eatery. After a few minutes a second barista delivers his order.

As he perches his nose above the hot green steam wafting from the mug, he glances at the door. The third time it opens his heart jumps. His vision locks onto the tallish woman in a grey flannel coat, charcoal stockings and burgundy riding boots. She darts her eyes until their pupils meet and acknowledges with a half-smile. Chase rises. He has agonized all morning as to how he should greet her. *Hug? Hug and kiss? No, no kiss. Handshake? Yeah, a handshake. No, that's too informal. Shit, she's here.*

"Hey, Jenae," he says.

She places a stuffed leather handbag on an empty seat.

"Hey," she says. She initiates a polite hug. Their cheeks touch. Their torsos do not. She leaves a generous space between their belt buckles. As she breaks the greeting, she rubs her jaw.

"Scratchy right?" Chase says. "I keep a light carpet of stubble nowadays."

"Carpet of stubble?" Jenae chuckles. "Still have a way with words I see. The beard is a good look for you. It goes with this whole smart casual thing you got going. Pinstriped shirt, tweed vest, blue jeans. Oh, and are those red Chuck Taylors? Chase Archibald is actually wearing sneakers? If you still go by Chase that is."

Well, she's sure pleasant. Cracking jokes? Going better than I expected.

"Yes, I still use Chase…but as a nickname. Tevarus *Chase* Huxley. And thanks, you look great yourself. Chic…gorgeous. Oh, let me get you something. You still don't drink coffee, right?"

"Some things do change you know," she says.

"Oh. My bad. Okay, what kind of cof—?"

"But not that," she says.

Chase shakes his head with a smile. He motions for AJ to bring another of his usual.

Jenae removes her hat and jacket. Her curls have grown into long, sienna brown locs. They cascade down the middle of her spine.

"This is a nice place," Jenae says.

"When you replied to my email saying you had moved to Jersey City I figured we could meet here in Essex County. I had moved out of the city too, after...well, after—"

"—After that mess called the Chase Archibald story?" she says.

Chase gives a sheepish nod just as AJ brings Jenae's order.

"After things settled, the firm kept their offer and I took the promotion in D.C. But that's government work. I missed the social justice. Life is too short to work a job—even a great paying one—that your heart isn't into. So I quit and started my own practice in J.C."

Jenae lathers a morsel of the butter biscuit with a scoop of apricot jam and swallows.

"Mmmm, Oh...oh my God, this melts in your mouth."

"I'm glad you like it. I wasn't sure you'd respond to my email."

"Well, after you went full stalker mode on me, and came to my job, I blocked your number and ignored all your emails."

"I wouldn't say I was a *stalker*, stalker."

"*Stalker*, stalker? There are levels to stalkery?"

"Well you seem to be okay with me now. You showed up."

"Presence isn't acceptance. Jury is still out," she says.

One of Jenae's locs flops between her blouse.

"Your hair got really long," he says.

"*Now* it is. I did the big chop after we broke up."

"Why do women always do that?"

"Why do men always makes us *want* to? But shifting gears... what do you do now?"

"A few things. I freelance write. I have a flash fiction app that readers subscribe to, I do motivational speaking at colleges. But since I can't pass a background check, I no longer teach."

"Oh, that reminds me. Whatever happened with Devantay?"

"Honestly, I don't know. I had Tanaka ask around for me. The home said Devantay ran off and never came back. Losing him is one of the regrets I write about in my memoir."

"Memoir?"

"Yes. I wanted to confront my truths. Tell my real story."

"That's why you contacted me? To tell the real story?"

"I just…Jenae. I never meant to hurt you. You deserve to know the real story."

Jenae raises her finger.

"Let's not discuss what I *deserved* or this hot ass tea may end up someplace else."

Chase takes a shy sip from his mug.

"Listen, you devastated me. But in talking to some of my sister-girls? There's a lot of you Chase Archibalds running from your Tevarus Huxleys. Your inner demons. Not everyone was as creative about it as you were. But honestly, there aren't too many men under forty that can truly understand a woman. In your twenties and thirties you're clueless. Over forty? Eh, you seem to do a bit better."

"Sooo…you're like…seeing someone over forty now?"

"Seriously? That's what you got from what I just said?"

"No, no, no."—*Damn, that was stupid*—"Jenae, I'm just really sorry for what I did."

"I'm sure you are. But I didn't come here for an apology."

Chase leans in, "I need you to know that I wasn't a child mo—"

"Child molester?"

Chase grits his teeth as he scans the room for eavesdroppers.

"Yeah, I know you weren't," she says.

"Maybe you *believe* I wasn't. But you don't know the real story."

"Oh no, not just because you say so. I learned that lesson."

Chase bristles at her not-so-subtle reminder.

"I started to research Tevarus Huxley the moment I was able to stop crying and blaming myself for being so stupid."

"You researched me?"

"Hell yes. I needed to know who I fell in love with. So I poured over the documents in the envelope that outed you. I saw you were really from Savannah, not Boston. Your Dad was a drill sergeant in the army. And he took that attitude home with him. Stern, unloving. And your mom had substance abuse and mental health issues."

"She was never there for me even when she was sober and lucid. My father's only emotions were anger and resentment. Hell, he never even visited me in prison. Someone else was more of a Dad."

"Angelo Hickson?"

"Dang, you found out about Bam too?"

"Women are experts at forensics, Chase. Bam had a long rap sheet. Racketeering, Ponzi schemes, illegal gambling, identity theft and fraud. He was charged for kidnapping and a prison murder too but it didn't stick. I figured he created the Chase Archibald identity."

Chase doesn't respond. He raises his tea mug for a hot sip.

"It's okay. A guy like Bam Hickson? You don't confirm what you do or don't know about him. But here's why I agreed to see you today. In my research I found out that you should never have been charged with a sex crime in the first place, let alone convicted of one."

Chase perks up.

"What do you mean?"

"I found out that you were a star quarterback at Cottonwood Regional High School. You even had an offer to USC right?"

"Yeah. And my father wouldn't even meet the coaches."

"So here's where it gets interesting. High school football in the South is like a religion."

"You're not kidding. Our stadium could seat 25,000 easy."

"And then came the night you beat your crosstown rivals, General Lee High, for the state championship."

"I threw seven touchdowns. That night was awesome until—"

"Until the party right? A few weeks after your 18th birthday."

"Yeah. That damn party. And that damn girl."

She rifles through several folders in her satchel.

"You brought research with you?"

"How many times do I have to prove how dope a lawyer I am?"

"Continue," he says.

"So the party was at your running back's house. There was a girl there. Blonde, blue-eyes and captain of General Lee's cheerleading team. And she was all over you. In court docs she admits she was flirting, initiating kisses, rubbing on your…*stuff*, and frankly just glued to you all night. And she wasn't inebriated. One thing leads to another and you guys go into an empty bedroom and have sex."

"Consensual, Jenae. Consensual!"

"Yes, Chase I realize that. But the girl was only fifteen *and* she attended the rival high school you just beat."

"But I didn't *know* she was fifteen, Jenae. I thought she was my age. She said she was a senior, and she looked like it. She even talked about how she applied to USC too. Jenae, if you would have seen her there's no way you would say she was a fifteen year old…*child*."

"Well, by that Monday rumors spread in both high schools that you broke a record with *another* touchdown that night."

"And that's when my problems started. Aside from being football rivals, her father was a county politician."

"An assemblyman to be exact. Politics, power, and good ol' boy racism regarding sex between a black male and a white female. When he found out he pressured her into accusing you of rape. A false accusation number one, and most certainly not child molestation."

Chase shifts in his chair. He curls his lips into his mouth and rubs his hands together.

"Chase, I know this is uncomfortable for you. But here's the thing. Teens have consensual sex all the time. And there was already a law on the books that should have been applied to your case. It's called the Romeo and Juliet exception."

Chase's eyes pop.

"Yeah, I bugged out too. Romeo and Juliet exceptions are when you have two teenagers who engage in consensual sex, but they are close in age. States differ but in Georgia, the female has to be either fourteen or fifteen and the male can be no older than eighteen. The girl in your case actually turned sixteen that following week. Your age difference was really only two years and three months. The prosecutor shouldn't have charged you at all, and probably would not have, if politics, race and sports tribalism weren't present."

"Unbelievable," Chase says.

"And to top it off, you had the kickback judge that sentenced you to five years."

"The kickback judge?"

"Judge Howard Steingardt. He was your judge at trial. Didn't you see him in the news last week? He got convicted on corruption charges. When I heard his name it jogged my memory about your case. I did this research after we broke up so I had forgotten all about him. Steingardt was getting kickbacks from private prisons. He would sentence young black boys to their institutions in exchange for a payoff. They called it *boys for bucks*."

"This is the nightmare all over again," Chase says.

"Now, in your case you were sent to a state facility so you weren't a part of the kickback scandal. But guess what? *All* of

Steingardt's cases are now being audited. So whether I wanted to see you again or not, I felt I had to. I had new information that could hopefully clear your name. Your real name."

Chase leans back to process this waterfall of information. Jenae plops a dollop of dark amber honey into her cup. A hush in the conversation reveals the twangy strings and organ riffs of Al Green's *Love and Happiness* streaming above them. Chase swirls his spoon around his matcha tea. He stirs and stirs and stares and stirs.

"Chase?"

"I'm here. I'm just...just processing. Jenae...you're amazing. After everything I put you through you still did all of this for me?"

She slurps her tea and cracks a tiny smile at the brim.

"So, what's the title of your memoir?" she says.

"It's called, *Chasing Tevarus: How I found my truth in a lie.*"

Jenae lifts an eyebrow.

"Interesting."

"So you understood my situation...how I got a raw deal."

"Yes, I did. It was quite a relief to be honest. It confirmed that you *weren't* the monster I was led to believe you were. I was even considering taking you back."

His expression brightens.

"You were? So, what stopped you?"

Jenae pauses, sips her tea and smiles. It's the kind of smile you make when you're about to ask a question you know the answer to. She scrapes her manicured fingernail on the rim of the mug and asks her next question without lifting her eyelids to speak.

"Is there anything you plan on leaving *out* of your memoir?"

"Out?...Oh, if you're worried about me writing anything that would hurt your career—"

"No, that's not what I mean? Your memoir is about the truth, right? Your truth. So is there anything you're going to leave out? Perhaps something you may have kept hidden, even from me?"

Chase still knows Jenae. She's asking for a reason. As he combs through the memories of those *Eugene days,* Jenae's face shines with hope. But Chase refuses to come clean. He won't be transparent.

"I'm sorry, I don't know what you mean."

Her anticipation turns to disappointment. That feeling you get when you're rooting for your player to hit the game winning shot and he clanks the ball off the backboard.

She sighs. "Okay, Chase...okay."

She continues.

"So my research exonerated you in my eyes. I thought about whether I should take you back and who to ask for an opinion. At first I thought about Tanaka but he was your boy. He would tell me to take you back no matter what you did. Then I said...why not call the person who has known Chase the longest? Talk to Andrea."

Chase fidgets.

"Andrea? I haven't spoken to her since everything blew up. She resigned from the university, moved out of Brooklyn and never returned my calls or texts either. I assumed she must have gotten one of those packages and didn't want to have anything to do with me."

"No, I don't think that was quite the reason. So I sought her advice because the two of you were such good friends. Of course didn't know just *how* good of a friend until she invited me for a chat."

"A chat?"

"Yes, a chat."

"She wasn't drinking was she?"

"Yup," Jenae says, with emphasis on the *puh* sound.

Chase's respiration ratchets.

"So we get to talking and she reveals something you never shared with me. The two of you used to be a couple. Engaged in fact."

"Uh, Jenae I—"

"I mean, girlfriend was going on and on about all the vacations you used to go on and how you used to lay it down in the bedroom."

"Look, Jenae. I—"

"And neither of you saw fit to mention this cozy history between you two. And then you maintain this coziness as a *friendship*—[she uses air quotes]—after I come into the picture?"

"My relationship with Andrea ended before you and I—"

Jenae wags her finger.

"Eh, eh, eh. Not done yet. I could see the wine was affecting her like truth serum so I filled her glass to the top. Bottoms up. She went off on you like a drunk Denzel in Training Day. *He gonna toss me aside? Propose to some OTHER chick? In MY muh-muh-fuckin' loft?*"

"Jenae, listen."

"I mean can you blame her? I know men can do some dumb shit but damn, Chase. How are you going to propose to your current girl in your *ex*-girl's house? Where they do that at?"

Chase tries to jump in.

"Oh no, boo-boo. Write this down. This will be great for your little book," she says, fanning her fingers at his palms. "So she tells me about that thug Eugene—who I later discovered was Bam's son—and this baby mama maker, scheme of his."

"Jenae, I was being blackmailed."

"Oh, I know. It didn't take long for me to piece that Eugene was blackmailing you about your identity. I remembered that crazy call from the lady with the bad Dominican accent too. And even with Andrea telling me all of this I *still* could've taken you back."

Chase looks astounded.

"I know. Crazy right? That's just it. It was so damn crazy…it actually made sense. You loved me. And you did all this because you wanted to keep your perfect life with the woman you loved."

"Yes, exactly. That was all I was trying to do."

Jenae swallows the last of her apricot biscuit with a final sip of tea.

"But there's just one little thing. Andrea took videos."

I forgot all about those damn recordings, Chase thinks to himself.

"So we're in her living room. She's trying to get on some cloud storage website to show me a video. She's totally wasted, mind you. Kept pulling up photos of Los Angeles real estate properties. She eventually found the videos though."

Chase tries to interrupt again. Jenae just cuts him off.

"The first one was hilarious. That chick was bat shit crazy. Then the lesbians. They were a trip. That one chick clocked you good. You were digging the pretty shorty though weren't you? Be honest?"

"Jenae, it wasn't like that. You saw I didn't follow through."

"But then there was that last video. The pretty bohemian."

"Last video?" Chase says.

She takes out her cellphone and starts thumbing.

"Jenae a lot has changed. Just let me—"

"Aaand press send. Done. I just sent it to you."

She then goes in her bag and takes out a trove of her Tevarus Huxley research documents for Chase. She rises, tightens her coat strap, and pops her collar.

"Jenae where are you going? Let's finish talking about this."

"We are finished. I came to help you. Give these docs to your lawyer. They'll help clear your name. Chase, I came here to help you but I also came because I needed to confront what I was avoiding. You. I needed to see if you had *truly* changed. I got my answer."

"But Jenae you know everything. Just give me a second ch—"

"—Chance? We all deserve second chances. I believe in them. But sometimes that second chance has to come from someone else."

Jenae walks to his chair. She cups Chase's face and slowly presses her lips to his. Her kiss is a sweet flood of the familiar. Her savory moistness. The feathery puffs from her nostrils exhaling on his skin. He could stay in this moment forever. But a moment is never a forever. With a gentle *lip-pop* Jenae releases. She rubs her thumbs on his cheeks. And doesn't speak. She smiles her goodbye. Chase monitors as Jenae exits onto the boulevard. Once again, she's gone.

Chase steeps in his chair like cold tea in an empty mug. *How could you let her slip away again?* He meanders his gaze. An old man uses a magnifying glass to read the *Star-Ledger*. A woman in bantu braids steps on stage with a guitar case and a stool. A hijab wearing coed, in a Montclair State hoodie, is highlighting her textbook. Chase sighs as he pulls out his laptop and checks his email. New Message:

From: JMDixon@51mail...
Subject: You're Still "Chase"-ing

There's no message. Just a link to a video. He clicks it. The video appears to have been recorded from atop a woman's dresser. Rayne Chimes appears in the frame. Her head is wrapped in a bath towel. Her skin glistens. She's cradling a cell phone and talking into her palms apparently unaware that she's being recorded:

"Dear Video Diary. Today is February 23rd. You already know about the conception plan I set up through my cousin Gregory. I paid to meet a guy named Chase and my reasons for wanting to have a child in this manner. Well Diary, Chase came over last night. Our vibe was perfect. Spiritual, sensual, holistic. He was sweet, attentive, passionate. And he *listened* to me. Something

THE DONOR

most men don't do enough with women. He listened to my hopes, my dreams, my desires. I mattered to him. He treated me like I was the *only* woman in the world. I mean, I know he has someone else. He's engaged to this lawyer. And he loves her. Just like I love my Ilyas. But last night? Last night, we loved *each other*. And soon I'll have something special to remind me of Chase forever and ever. Well Diary, signing off until next time. It's your girl...Rayne Chimes."

Chase drops his head to the table. He is dumbfounded as to how there could be a video. He remembers leaving the teddy bear face down on the floor. But then it dawns on him. Rayne said she knew the *perfect place* to put the stuffed animal. That place must have been on her bedroom dresser. And since Andrea apparently never stopped recording...it captured Rayne's message. Chase wants to hurry a reply to Jenae and plead his case. He composes his thoughts just as the guitarist plays an acoustic version of *Ex-Factor* by Lauryn Hill. He pauses his reply... *No, not 'til you truly get right.*

Chase closes his email. He instead opens his completed four hundred page memoir. He selects the entire text of the document and hits delete. The page is blank. He smiles. The cursor blinks, patiently awaiting a command. Chase cracks his knuckles, curls his fingers and types a brand new title:

```
Chase Archibald
I Die At The End
A Memoir


Tevarus Huxley
```

Insights By The Author for Readers and Book Clubs

The Donor was inspired by my interest in exploring two main themes related to choice. The first theme revolves around running from your past and ignoring unresolved issues.

There's an easter egg in the first chapter. Did you catch it? Chase is teaching from Edgar Allan Poe's *A Telltale Heart.* Just before he dismisses the class he says: "And remember this theme: Whenever you try to run from yourself, it is your *self* that will always catch up." That is essentially Chase's fatal flaw. He kept running. Perhaps you caught the metaphor being repeated by Chase jogging and always running into Miss Pat who is a metaphor for the past. I used Eugene's blackmail to show the difficulty of choice. Chase's world was built on a lie. He could have challenged Eugene. But if you were being blackmailed and if you didn't comply you'd lose your family, your career, significant other, everyone you loved…guaranteed…what would you do? Is the choice really that easy?

A second theme in *The Donor* revolves around conception and womanhood. The women Eugene recruited all wanted to conceive and have a child but weren't in a conventional situation to do so. I conducted a survey of 104 women before I wrote the novel. One of the questions was: You have no significant other. For whatever reason [clock ticking, desire for motherhood, family expectations] you want to have a child. Given a choice between an anonymous donor from a fertility clinic, or engaging in the natural act of copulation, which would you choose? Two-thirds said they'd prefer the act. That made me think about the power of the desire to conceive [naturally] but also the social pressures we place on women to do so. We don't do that with men. I thought that idea would make for great storytelling.

Both of these themes are connected because they ultimately boil down to the choices we make and the consequences of our actions.

Thank You For Reading
Do These Four Things

1. WRITE a review on your favorite book retailer's site
2. SUBSCRIBE to Brother Dash www.brotherdash.com
3. SHARE pics of you and a link to the book on social media
4. PURCHASE other books buy Brother Dash

Other Books By Brother Dash

Sweet Mojo

One Man's Descent Through Danger & Delight

Book 1: The Mojo Series

A Harlem heartthrob croons his way into a steamy village of vixens. But all hell breaks loose when they discover the song he sings, hides the poison he brings.

Made in the USA
Middletown, DE
17 April 2018